Aleister Crowley MI5

Richard C McNeff

Mandrake

Copyright © 2021 Richard C McNeff

First paperback Edition

Previously published 2004 as *Sybarite among the Shadows*

All rights reserved. No part of this work may be reproduced or utilized in any form by any means electronic or mechanical, including *xerography, photocopying, microfilm*, and *recording*, or by any information storage system without permission in writing from the publishers.

Published by
Mandrake
PO Box 250
OXFORD
OX1 1AP (UK)

'Probably the finest modern novel featuring
Aleister Crowley.' *Lashtal*

'Few historical novels so firmly rooted in fact can boast demonic invocations, buggery and "the ghastly shade of the Rector of Skiffley, recently devoured by a lion at the funfair". But seldom does an author decide to wrap his narrative around the exploits of someone like occultist and sex-fiend Aleister Crowley. Set in 1936, this tells of Victor "Vicky" Neuburg, a former acolyte of Crowley's, who receives a visit from Dylan Thomas. The two of them set off for the Surrealist Exhibition, where they find Salvador Dali "wearing a deep-sea diver's suit decorated with green plasticine hands" and Wyndham Lewis "attired in a fedora and long black cloak". It's all remarkably accurate stuff. After the exhibition, they trawl Bohemian London until they meet Crowley, who is employed by MI5 as part of a plot involving Prince Edward and Wallis Simpson. Much more than a Who's Who of 1930s eccentrics ... this book shines a flickering light on the British avant-garde.' *Independent on Sunday*

'A swaggering romp of a novel. Plot by Buchan; characters by Beardsley; setting Art Deco — difficult to better that.' *Wormwood*

'Aleister Crowley, mountaineer, mage and magician, has been the basis for a number of fictional characters — Somerset Maugham's Oliver Haddo, M. R. James' Karswell, Anthony Powell's Scorpio Murtlock, Dennis Wheatley's Mocata and even Ian Fleming's Le Chiffre in the first James Bond story, *Casino Royale*. Rarely has he appeared in fiction as himself. Here, in a highly researched story he is himself in all his occult and charismatic glory — a manipulative, overbearing, bizarre yet compelling character. Fiction could hardly have invented him: he is a gift of a character to any novelist and Richard C McNeff has accepted him, unwrapped the parcel and given him his head.'

Martin Booth, author of *A Magick Life*

'Full of fascinating nuggets. Neuburg's crisis of identity with AC is very well observed.' Snoo Wilson, author of *I, Crowley*

'Crowley in this incarnation is vividly brought to life, illuminating both his attraction, and his parasitical dependence on others, like Neuberg, who he requires to do his bidding, see the visions he conjures up, and supply the readies. The milieu, too, is both more real and more glamorous, the Fitzrovia of old, haunted by painters, poets and hangers-on, and the notorious Gargoyle Club on Meard Street, where 1930s socialites smoked opium and rubbed shoulders – perhaps – with disgraced royalty.'
James Bridle, 'The Sybaritic British Empire'

'... a well-researched fictional account of the relationship between Crowley and Neuburg.' *Glossary of Thelema*

'The characterisation is quite subtle; so Dylan Thomas is comic and raucous, but – as a poet – ultimately earnest. Aleister Crowley remains a mysterious and ambivalent figure, and is certainly a more rounded character here than as Oliver Haddo (probably his best known fictional alter-ego). 1930s London is well depicted, with plenty of realistic period detail. This is an unusual and intriguing novel and an entertaining foray into an earlier, stranger England.'
Paul Kane, *Compulsive Reader*

Contents

I°	In the Swim	8
II°	The Phosphorescent Nephew	21
III°	Nina	37
IV°	Life No. 13	55
V°	La Tour Eiffel	75
VI°	Great Raven	96
VII°	Gargoyles	114
VIII°	The Forty-Three	138
IX°	Shadows of a Shade	151
X°	The Bornless Ones	172
XI°	The Oracle of Dawn	187
Afterword		204

To Astara, Lynne and Dick

I invoke Thoth, the Lord of Wisdom and
Of Utterance,
The God that cometh forth from the veil.
O thou! Majesty of Godhead! Wisdom-crowned Thoth!
Lord of the Gates of the Universe! Thee, thee, I invoke.

The Invocation of Thoth

1°
In the Swim

On a rooftop the wreckage of the front end of a London bus was still smoking. The metal was scorched, and along the buckled side panel, an advertisement for Capstan Full Strength was appositely singed. Wondering how it had been blown there, Vicky looked from bus to sky and saw tethered over London scores of barrage balloons nosing their way through banks of magnificent cloud.

A voice was calling, banishing the images that had left him white-faced and tensed in the armchair. As usual, the vision had possessed a film-like quality, and it was with a less than cinematic precision that the familiar articles of his study, the chipped desk, the portrait of Chaucer with its worm-holed frame, the tattered folios on the shelves, reassembled before him. Victor Neuburg was a bony individual with a head too big for his body, a prominent nose, perforated by eczema, and brown hair shorn so close the curls were only once more beginning to unfurl. He was wearing a dark green shirt, a tea-stained tartan tie, fawn corduroy breeches flecked with cigarette burns, and after a careless square of skin, rucked grey socks that disappeared into a pair of dilapidated slippers.

He lived in his study these days. Occasionally, there were the visions for company, which alarmed him much less than they had used to. If anything, they brought some relief from the tedium. Besides these, he had only memories: the chain chafing his neck as his master led him across the Algerian desert beneath fountains of stars, or the uncanny light dancing with shadow in the Paris hotel room where they had invoked Jupiter (the face of the God, awesome and unbearable). Nothing remarkable would ever happen again. His adventures were finished, as were the receptions and public readings, the mentions in the press, the eager young poets vying for praise. He had become the curator of his youth.

The voice called again, the door swung open, and Runia hovered on the threshold like a wet weekend.

'You'll be late for the printers!' Her tone was curt these days. She was losing faith.

'Is it today, my dear?' bleated Vicky.

He was forcing himself to rise when the doorbell rang. They both looked surprised. There were hardly any visitors these days. Runia went to answer it and returned a few moments later. She had that pinched look on her handsome features that unsettled him so much.

'Dylan's here,' she said in a flustered tone. 'Drunk I shouldn't wonder. I told him you were working, but he insisted on coming in.'

More nervous of her than of his visitor, Vicky went out into the hall, which in turn gave onto the conservatory.

Dylan was standing by the bookcase squinting at the titles. He had grown a little plumper in the year since Vicky had seen him but was still cherubic, his nest of curls tousled, though not by wind, for it was one of those temperate days in early June when London flings off its overcoat and apes Marseilles. Instead, his unshaven chin, bloodshot eyes and rumpled blue check suit, with the telltale bulge in the right-hand pocket, spoke of a night of it. Nevertheless, something in his look seemed haunted by more than drink.

'Do you think a man can read another's mind, Vicky?' he demanded, without preamble, in that singsong voice in which only the lilt was Welsh. 'I mean gambol about, rummaging like a burglar?'

The first question would have sufficed, but Dylan as ever was flush with words. It had been more than eighteen months since he had outgrown Vicky's now-defunct Poet's Corner in the Sunday Referee. The Adelphi and Eliot's Criterion currently championed his verse. Several critics, including Edith Sitwell, the great arbitress of the new, had hailed his first book Eighteen Poems, whose publication Vicky had fostered, as nothing short of a miracle. The cub was becoming a lion.

'I was in the Swiss last night,' he went on a little breathlessly, 'in cahoots with this Polish girl I'd met at Pop Kleinfield's. We had put back a few, and she was laying into me something chronic. I had heard that sort of guff before, so I just stood there doodling on the bar. I noticed a man sitting in the gloom. He was staring up at me. Large fellow, thickset, looked like a stockbroker, apart from his head, which was shaven, oh, and the hands, which were very dainty. In one, he was miffing a brandy; with the other, deliberately, as though he wanted me to notice, he took a pen from his jacket and began drawing on a napkin. The cheeky bugger's mimicking me, I thought.'

'Shaven head, you say?' said Vicky, trying unsuccessfully to conceal his excitement.

'Apart that is from a little horn of hair, which I noticed when he lumbered over like an eclipse and tried to hypnotise me with the pin on his swaying tie. It was a large ebony brooch, bearing the head of a stork-like bird with a long bill curved like a boomerang. Moreover, did he stink! There was this cloying scent like cheap perfume. "I think we artists should compare productions," he wheezed, and waved his drawing under my nose. Bugger me black if he hadn't drawn the same as me!'

Dylan was too good a writer not to pause there. Sunlight was embossing the goldfish as they broke the surface of the fountain pool. A bird chose that moment to sing. Vicky asked the obvious.

'We'd both drawn a face. A Pan-like face a stranger might have called it, but anyone who knew your bony nose and tumbling locks, which I see you have now had shorn, would have taken it as yours. He had drawn your curls like pricks, I, of course, like hyacinths, but the absent sitter was the same. That is why I had to come. No offence, I hope, Vickybird.'

Vicky found it disturbing to hear his old nickname again. It reminded him of the days when the house had been full of callers. He asked Dylan if he had discovered the identity of the man, hoping he had not, and that after a few platitudes about Telepathy and the Ether, he could send him on his way.

'The greasy Pole said she'd met him in the Wheatsheaf.' Dylan uttered the name. Though he mispronounced the first syllable, rhyming it with 'crown' not 'crow', Vicky was grateful Runia was not in range to hear a word so long outlawed in their house.

'The brooch bore the ibis head of Thoth,' he said hurriedly, as though presenting his credentials. 'The scent was the unguent Ruthvah, so rich in musk that horses whinny when they smell it.'

'I almost did myself,' said Dylan. 'But why had he drawn your face?'

Vicky moved closer to the bookcase as though among the many volumes on magic it contained a solution would be furnished to this riddle - which, in a sense, it might.

'I was his student for five years before the Great War. He was not then as you see him now. He was a poet of great promise.'

He turned to the shelves, and after a little time, for his habits were louche and this disorder extended to his library, he took down a folio-size volume, which he held before Dylan. It was The Oxford Book of Mystical Verse, an anthology more prestigious than any the Welshman had yet been in. Instead of reading one of the three poems it contained by Crowley, however, Vicky extracted a yellowing sheet which bore, in scrawled and rapid autograph, an early draft of The City of God, a poem which he had always considered one of the Beast's finest. Unfolding it, he began to recite in the sonorous voice he reserved for readings.

'Verse,' barked Dylan after about five lines. It was the worst judgement in his canon.

Somewhat unwillingly, Vicky agreed. 'We were poetasters,' he confessed, 'besotted by obsolescent words and antiquated forms. With you it is so different.'

Dylan, who was not big headed, ignored the flattery.

'Besides what meaning does it have? It's just a bouquet of pretty lyrics.'

'Coming from you I find that most ostrobogulous.'

This curious word was to be Vicky's sole legacy to the English language. Even today, certain dictionaries define it as meaning "pornographic". An inventor is permitted liberties, however, and Vicky used it for anything he found odd or contradictory.

Dylan groaned. 'You're not one of those who think I sit down with a tumbler of Bass and reel off torrents of heady spiel? Accuse me of muddle-headedness, if you will, cruelty to rhyme, a top-heavy imagery that sways like Babel, but please get one thing straight - every line is meant to be understood.'

'As is his,' countered Vicky. 'However, to understand The City of God you have to know something of the Cabbala and the Splendid Lights.'

'I saw a few of them in the Plough last night,' muttered Dylan.

'Picture a tree, which has at its crest a sphere of unbearable brilliance. Beneath it are nine more spheres, which end in this gloom where our spirits are imprisoned. Twenty-two Paths zigzag down like lightning bolts. Each is mirrored by forms as vague and treacherous as a tree reflected by the dank waters of a lake.'

Dylan blinked and gazed out at the garden wondering if beech or elm were the Tree of Life. 'It exists then, this Cable Wallah? I can slap it across the shoulders and bid it a hearty good day?'

'You can discover it through its attributes: planets, emotions, colours, things like that. The Cabbala is a frame of reference; a Pantacle that furnishes the glyphs needed to describe the universe.'

'I might just take a fancy to "glyph",' said Dylan, turning the word on his tongue like a wine buff savouring a rare vintage. 'So it was this you studied with Great Raven?'

Vicky chuckled at the pun. He had moved nearer to the window. Across the lawn, in a gap between the facing houses, a horse-drawn milk float was shambling down Belsize Road. Sunlight fleeced gold from the foil that sealed the bottles.

'And other forms of magic,' he said.

Dylan looked at him askance. The word summoned vampires and hobgoblins. He had a child's fear of such things. 'Did it work this magic?' he demanded

Vicky thought of the forms of shadow, or the shadows of form - he had never discovered which; of Mars whom he had danced down. He remembered that sly and shifting shape they had summoned, mouthing its obscenities in the desert; and last of all Ione, always pale, in death more so, the blood caking her waist-length tresses like an inferior henna.

'Only too well,' he said.

Hurriedly, the Welshman pulled a bottle of pale ale out of his pocket and, after further rummaging, opened it with a penknife. He took a deep swig. 'Like the way he knew what I was drawing,' he said so breathlessly that beer mingled with the spittle. 'Or the feeling you can get in a shadowy room with a worm of light staining the window, when you fix your eyes on the face of another. Slowly the jaw sags, the brow merges with the cheeks, and the face is an eerie white oval hemmed by darkness. Then new features appear: the dribbling maw of a goat, fangs, eyebrows that curl upwards like the devil's tail. '

'It was exactly such a face I saw in the desert a quarter of a century ago.'

'And who might that have been, dear?' Runia had entered as noiselessly as the goldfish in the pool.

Already one name had been uttered that had lain like a curse on Vicky these past twenty years; now he was called upon to pronounce another so terrible it should never be said; one, furthermore, whose bearer knew him and might by its utterance be summoned back. The bottle Dylan was toasting her with, however, diverted Runia. Vicky observed her lips purse, widen to a "Dis ...", stopper the "gusting", then say instead: 'I hope you're not going to drink that here. Victor finds the smell repugnant.'

Tight-lipped, Dylan stood there, the bottle dangling in space. Runia must cup her farts under the blanket in the fond delusion their stink resembled the aroma of Wordsworth's daffodils, he decided.

'I really don't...,' Vicky began, but Runia put paid to his "mind" with her more forceful own.

'You know how the fumes upset you, Victor!'

It had been like this for seven years now; despotism more total than any he had endured under Crowley. Once the Beast had bidden him to avoid saying "I" for a week, making him punish each transgression by a self-inflicted slash with a razor. However, Runia, "progressive" Runia, had gone one step further: she forbade him to be himself at all. Like a colonial administrator dealing with surly natives, her tyranny cloaked itself in the fiction that all was in his best interests. A visit to a shoe shop resulted in the assistant asking her, not him, if the shoe fitted; a request for his opinion would invariably elicit hers, couched, of course, as authentic Neuburg. Runia, however, paid the bills. Her income had financed Comment. They had launched the magazine the previous year after The Sunday Referee had lurched down market and his column been withdrawn. It was about this she began to speak, in a tone that made Vicky cringe.

'Victor took you up, young man; he first published you. Without him, you would still be twiddling your thumbs in Swansea. Yet when he needed you, you let him down.'

Vicky spluttered. This just was not true. Dylan had sent them a story and several poems for no fee at a time when he could sell his work and needed, as he always needed, money.

'Oh, there might have been a few droppings from your table,' she conceded. 'But in the elevated circles you now move in you could have done so much more.'

'True enough,' agreed Dylan cheerily, who when attacked often resorted to ridicule, even if he made himself its object. 'I'm well in with the racketeers. Riding shotgun with Pope Eliot and Dame Sitwell is I; glutted with money and fame by the muses, and invitations galore to academies of the Super-real. "Tell me, Mister Inkwell, what was your first word? Is Germany an ogre? Do you believe Shakespeare was a woman?" Lobster for tea, white wine every night, a shrine in Westminster Abbey, and a pit of black earth beneath it.'

Typically, Dylan had ended with his shield against hubris – death.

'The function of poetry is to address the higher realms of spirit and nature. It should enhance man, not debase him,' insisted Runia. 'Your poems mostly make no sense, and when they do the import is disgusting - all that doggerel about worms and wombs.'

Vicky had himself castigated Dylan in the pages of The Referee for the excessive number of references to worms in Eighteen Poems. His school, that of Rossetti and Swinburne, favoured lilies over tadpoles, but practically every poem submitted to Poet's Corner in the wake of Dylan's slim volume had had a worm or maggot in it. He was far from happy with Runia's attack, however. He was convinced the Welshman was authentic, and was about to say so when the poet himself stepped in. Runia could have made fun of his liking for loud suits, his unkempt hair, his size, and Dylan would have happily seconded her. In attacking his poetry, however, she had maligned the one thing he considered sacred. Taking a defiant swig of Burton's, and then drawing himself up to his full five feet six, he laid into them:

'You provided a lot of sheep with Horlicks, eh Vicky. Odes to Persian cats, lines like 'Violet skies all rimmed in tune,' send Creative Timeservers like you into spasms of bliss, though they're nothing more than tears streaking the powdered cheeks of a ghastly Pantomime Dame. The truth is your tipsy muse is never tanked up enough to push the buttons nor sober enough to tell anybody anything real or true!' With a theatrical flourish, Dylan indicated the little platform Runia had had erected before the French windows, from which aspiring poets, such as he himself and David Gascoyne, no longer recited, and declaimed in his actor manager's voice: 'I call on Theobald Cocaine to recite his Sonnet to Watercress.'

How changed was this exuberant man from the gangling youth Vicky had summoned to his office two summers before in order that the Referee's editor could grill him - for nobody could understand how one so young could produce such marvellous work. This difference, Vicky sensed, was not just the result of celebrity or drink. Perhaps he had met a woman who possessed a quality that completed the partial in his being: Dylan's yolk had found an egg - an excruciating image but one that came without apology.

'I have never heard anything viler in my life,' said Runia, though in fact she had, when she first met Vicky and he had confessed to her his adventures with the Beast. 'Of course, not all Victor published was of the same evenness. He was nobly seeking to lend a helping hand...'

Poet's Corner had been his nursery Vicky wanted to say. He had always found it hard to pluck out weeds.

'A hand to whom?' spat Dylan now all venom. 'Anyone with a smattering of the English and a watering can of images to sprinkle over their flowery lines. They could not leave their droppings in a private spot. You had to provide a public convenience for them to dump them in!'

Runia was no match for this brilliant bile. In seven years, Vicky had never seen such a pleading look on her Valkyrie face as that she gave him now. He began to stutter a reproach, but Dylan was ahead of them.

'Throwing me out is a popular hobby among many of my acquaintances, but before you do, let me tell you I have always loathed your notion that poetry's a sort of milk pudding of word-tinkling designed to lull the listener. I want to make symphonies out of the blood of the womb, to unwrap the winding sheet and find an overture. You blubber on about some lofty region where poetry attains its pinnacle. You say the artist must be a Socialist and sermonise accordingly. The artist is under no such obligation; in fact, he is not required to do anything at all. The nutshell of image is his kingdom. He has only one boundary and that is the mightiest of them all - the curb of form.'

'Formlessness is precisely what we complain of,' said Runia. 'You and your fellow Apocalyptics indulge in such antics with rhyme and employ such horrid metaphors that everything good or noble is left out.'

'I am not a scientist distilling words in a test tube and boiling up images with a Bunsen Burner in order to invent some outrageous effect - that article you wrote about me in the Referee was sheer bilge, Vicky. My little breakthroughs are not the spoils of theory or a school, but of the fact that I have no other way of negotiating the brambles and barbed wire of the pit I burrow in. My theme is vermin and putrefaction, you see, because I believe man is at root wicked and life a maggot. I will tip poetry into its grave tomorrow and dance on its tumours.'

Dylan moved to the door and huffed through it. There was a moment of scrambling in the hall, and then the front door slammed.

Runia turned to Vicky, her relief palpable. Now they were to collude, scold Dylan for his dreadful behaviour and then, after much twittering, blame it on the beer and find it in their generous hearts to forgive him. However, something stopped Vicky, something more than the scorn with which Dylan had blasted their circle. Damozel, their tortoiseshell cat, was nibbling at some half-eaten kippers on a plate beneath the table. A warming pan lay alongside these, as useless on this hot June day as his contribution to English letters.

He had always craved to be in the swim. It was that desire that had driven him to Crowley. However, that river had taken him over rapids from which he had been flung, first to the Western Front, and then to Sussex, where he had spent the twenties printing fine editions of his own poetry that no one had wanted to buy. Poet's Corner had given him another chance, but now that too had gone. The day stretched ahead with a chop for lunch, Marmite for tea and a trip to the printers to check the proofs of a volume that was to be the best of Comment, paid for by Runia, which no-one would read and no critic review; unless, of course, it were he himself under the ludicrous pseudonym Alfricobas, in a column loaned as a favour in The New English Weekly, in which, if he were honest, he should damn the contents as surely as Dylan had. Eliot, Auden, and perhaps Thomas himself were the rivers of his time. Compared to them Vicky was a pool of stagnant water choked by lilies. He belonged with those whose sole admirers were maggots.

With a resolve unnatural to him, he left the room and, as Runia squealed in the hall behind, exchanged his slippers for shoes and donned a Norfolk jacket, too hot and bothered for the season. He unlatched the door and loped down the steps.

The appalling discovery of his own insignificance was not all that drove him, however. For twenty-two years, he had been in hiding from a man whom he still could not decide was the best or worst that had ever lived. Crowley had ruined his life and killed his love Ione. It was believed when Vicky broke with him, that the Beast had cursed him and changed him into a camel - mistakenly, for it had been another animal. He was sure he was still the butt of jokes about this in the studios of Chelsea and Notting Hill; more crucially, several organs would not carry his work because of the stink. Yet when he looked back on his years with the Beast, he beheld a realm of colours, a city, if you like, of God. Everything after had been monochrome, and until that Thursday morning he had submitted as cheerfully as he could to the tyranny of Runia and the entirely humdrum. In debunking his muse, however, Dylan had alerted him to the possibility that the sole significance of his life resided with Crowley. Rogue and charlatan, rightfully vilified by the yellow press? Or the true prophet of the age whose greatest disciple he had been? And his Holy Guru was out there, in London, today! Vicky had been summoned by a doodle.

11°
The Phosphorescent Nephew

At the top of Boundary Road Dylan strolled jauntily, a green hat on his head. Even stretched out drunk upon a stranger's floor or flung bodily from a pub, he was exactly where Vicky wanted to be - in the swim. This was indeed Vickybird's last chance, which is why the interruption, when it came, was so excruciating.

'Gorgeous, ain't it?' a voice waylaid him.

Dylan had just turned left into the Finchley Road, but Vicky's old habit of chivalry made him pause, for the speaker was a woman, leaning over a hedge.

She had a saucy face, framed by hennaed hair, and was about forty. Her body still boasted a firm bust and shapely shoulders, beneath a blouse flecked in a tiger-skin pattern. They had noticed her in the area for about the last year. Runia, whom she had once accosted in the patisserie on College Parade, had judged her the wrong sort. This observation was borne out by her voice, which aspired to refinement but was betrayed by cockney tones as she went on:

'Bloomin' wonderful day for a spot of gardening.'

On any other occasion, Vicky would have been effusive in his admiration of the flowers she indicated with a sweep of her freckled arm, but his every pore was in motion.

She looked disapprovingly at him and tutted: 'What you're in such a hurry to find it might be better not to look for. I had a friend once, fine young man, up at Oxford, you know. He went searching for things that ain't permitted. Killed him in the end, it did. There are them only too glad to lead you up a blind alley.'

'I've never seen carnations quite that shade of pink before' said Vicky, sliding one foot forward onto the next paving.

'You've got the same look as my friend - you're as full of it as the birds with song. I will tell you something. There's only one thing worth being insatiable about – that's what you find between the sheets.'

Her lusty cackle pursued him as he moved off. An encounter Runia would not have approved of, he thought, and one besides that meant he might have lost Dylan. However, turning into the Finchley Road he saw the poet sauntering ahead. He caught up with him opposite the dairy alongside the Swiss Cottage Tavern. Dylan did not seem to welcome Vicky's appearance, and his erstwhile editor had eyes only for the hat. With a feather and cord band instead of a ribbon, it was in the Tyrolese style made fashionable by the King when Prince of Wales. Vicky had bought it, on Runia's insistence, at Dunn's in Piccadilly for a very serious two guineas. It still bore the dent on one side inflicted by a car that had run over it after it had blown off his head on a windy March morning beside Whitestone Pond.

'A gift from an admirer,' declared Dylan grandly. He was notorious for walking off with the clothing of anyone who had entertained him, a licence he also applied to money. Vicky began to frame a protest the poet forestalled by fishing in his pocket and bringing out a leaflet that he began waving about. On the cover, it bore a Greek statue wearing a bolero and holding a fan.

'Today is a great day,' Dylan declared,' one which will change the Capital Punishment forever. Stockbrokers will grow wings and take off from their office ledges; secretaries will copulate in the champagne cascading from the fountains of Trafalgar Square. For, this, yes this,' brandishing the paper, 'is an invitation to a New World.'

Things were falling into place, but with little thanks to Dylan. From the words printed beneath the torso, Vicky gleaned that the leaflet was an invitation to the opening of the International Exhibition of Surrealism. There had been warnings. A week before The Sunday Dispatch had announced "a storm over London" and spoken of invading madness. Now the great day had dawned.

'It's dreadfully easy to fall back into barbarism,' he said, 'as these modernists who are parleying with the mind's depths know.'

'You don't have to be a Surrealist to plumb the abyss, you know,' objected Dylan. 'And why shouldn't it be plumbed? Can there be no weeds in a poet's garden? Are we just here to water roses? To go all flower-faced and write lots of verses about the sun coming up?' Peering at Vicky's hurt features, Dylan removed the hat, and sweeping it towards his shoulder, made a little bow. 'O mighty Neuburg,' he declaimed, 'you must forgive me. Drink, an encounter with him they call the Beast, and the lubricious attentions of a cracker from Krakow have sabotaged my manners. Besides, I am not, nor ever have been a Surrealist. I intend every line to be a rasher of sense the reader can get his teeth into and have a good chew. So do come along. You need taking out of yourself. All that is required is a descent into metroland.'

In the swim again, with Dylan as his tug, Vicky was towed beneath the pagoda-like awning that shaded the entrance to the tube. Expecting no objection from the poet and receiving none, he fished in his pocket for the fare and bought two tuppenny tickets from a surly youth, half-asleep behind the counter.

The underground was something Vicky usually avoided. To his mind there was a grotesque air about the long tunnels ferrying rat-like commuters through the bowels of London, and the latest addition to the tube's armoury of mechanical wonders did nothing to alter his opinion. Dylan laughed as Vickybird hesitated before the moving staircase, of a type that had been recently installed at all the major stations in the metropolis. As it trundled down into the gloom, Vicky had visions of his leather heels trapped in the sinister gap between stairs and side, and the rest of him following, until he was spewed out like meat from a mincer. Dylan nudged him forward, and he was moving down, with the poet just behind doing his best to choke back the mirth Vickybird's discomfort had induced.

There had been one real improvement in the tube, however. The posters lining the hall at the bottom of the escalator were bright and full of verve. The Great Ziegfield, the hit film of the season, was advertised in lush, romantic colours, and the ship with seascape of the Cunard ad, inviting them to cruise the Western Mediterranean for thirty guineas, evoked Manet in its use of form and shade. It had taken Impressionism forty years to hit the High Street. Now Dylan and Vicky were off to see the monster it had spawned. On the platform, they waited for the train, smoking two of the Woodbines the poet had thoughtfully reminded Vickybird he possessed.

'Was the Beast really so different when you first met him?' he asked as the smoke curled upwards, forming veils in the lamplight. 'It's difficult to believe anyone would fall for him now.'

Dylan, true to form, had minted the right word. "Fall" it had been in several senses, plummeting down so far as to brush the lips of hell itself with Vicky's eager own. By unspoken accord, they had used "He", "the Beast", whatever euphemism sprang to mind so long as the word was not Crowley - a name formerly innocuous enough amongst his Plymouth Brethren forbearers, but one so loaded with associations now, its very utterance might damn them.

'When he first appeared in my rooms at Trinity,' Vicky said, 'he possessed a trim, athletic build and a fine-featured face that seemed to shine with a light quite alien to the hues of England in that golden autumn of 1909. He had visited China and India, had climbed mountains in the Himalayas and shot big game. The fact that he married such virile pursuits with the practice of magic was, if anything, a bonus. You see I was stumbling along the same road. Ever since I could remember, I had detested the normal. I had dabbled in Esperanto, vegetarianism, and the humanism of the Freethinker's Association. I had read Nietzsche and thought myself a superman. But each was a fad as quickly discarded as it had been taken up until I met Lord Boleskine.'

He could not help smiling at the incredulous way in which Dylan repeated the name. Anyone not wishing to say "Crowley" was spoilt for alternatives, so many were the aliases the Master Therion had coined for himself.

'He was a laird, he told me, with a house on the shores of Loch Ness. In his kilt, sporran and plaid jacket, he looked every inch the part. He came quite often after that. We would smoke weed in my rooms and travel on the astral. He gave me books to read, not just about magic, but works by Kant and Berkeley, and even Dostoevsky, who was then largely unknown. He wrote himself. Conrad had praised his short stories. Though you didn't like City of God, his poetry I thought sublime. He was widely published in reviews and anthologies. Trouble, however, was never far away. He was due to give a talk to the Free Thought Association at the university, but someone sent a letter to the authorities accusing him of the vice of Sodom and of being watched by the police of Europe. "Good, I shan't be burgled," was his response. Then he sent a letter to the father of Norman Mudd, the pathetic creature who had proposed him, accusing the Dean of Trinity of the same practices he had been charged with himself.'

'You could almost like the man!' exclaimed Dylan.

'Oh, never underestimate him. He has charm and wit, or at least he did. Another time, when I was with him up in Boleskine, he wrote to the Society for the Prevention of Prostitution in London complaining about how conspicuous loose women were in the area. The society sent an inspector who spent a dismal three weeks tramping round the bothies and then informed us he could not find even one. "I meant conspicuous by their absence," A.C. told him.'

Dylan let out a whoop of laughter. A train was approaching. Growl became roar as it sped down the tunnel from Finchley Road Station. Vicky felt compelled to put into a nutshell the allure that had warped his life, before this other beast pulled in.

'He told me through magic all the hypotheses of imagination can be proved. He spoke of man as a vertical line rising towards the union of all contraries above the abyss. Is it any wonder I was bewitched?'

He wanted to go on, but the tube-train deafened them both as it burst into the station. The red doors slid apart and entering the compartment, which was nearly empty, they slumped onto two seats. Dylan flicked his ash onto a floor already littered with butts and sweet wrappers. His action excited hostile looks from the two hikers sitting opposite. Typically, they wore berets, open-necked khaki shirts, potato-coloured shorts, and their waterproof rucksacks occupied the seats to either side. They were on their way to one of the great stations, where they would take a special rambler train that would drop them at a mystery destination in Kent or Sussex - perhaps even Steyning, where they could climb up to the crumbling dolmens of Vicky's beloved Chanctonbury ring. Refusing to be intimidated, Dylan threw his dog-end onto the floor and loudly demanded another 'Woodie' from his companion. 'I'm sure they'll soon find that cigarettes have a very beneficial effect on health.' He supported this prediction by a loud burst of coughing.

'The Medical Research Council has spent years exposing mice to different forms of smoke,' chipped in Vicky, oblivious to the hatred of the hikers. 'Their conclusion is that cigarette and traffic fumes are harmless.'

Dylan cast a look of withering scorn across the compartment.

At Baker Street they changed, crossing to the Bakerloo platform, which was unusually full for a Thursday morning. Here and there were extravagant deviations from normal dress. A young man in a sky blue suit festooned with seashells; another dressed as a harlequin; a woman with a hat shaped and numbered like a dice, distinguished the crowd, which was wealthier than average for it was a working day. The costume of the apparition who entered the crowded compartment at Oxford Circus, however, outmatched all others. She was wearing a white satin gown and a veil of roses that concealed her face. Long black gloves covered her hands, in one of which she carried a model human leg, of the type used for shop-window dummies, while the other cradled a raw pork chop. Admiration was excited in many faces, but in none more than Dylan's, who leaned across just as the train was pulling into Piccadilly Circus and complimented her on her lunch box. No reaction was discernible beneath the veil as the woman was carried by the crush out onto the platform. 'I think it's going to be a French letter day,' crowed Dylan, nevertheless, as they underwent the same translation.

Soon she was lost in the stream of people flowing towards the moving stairs and was nowhere to be seen in the oval hall above, with its gleaming new automaticket machines. Dylan pointed to the words above the chart, recording every train that passed through, which said "See how they run". The words seemed more appropriate to the passengers than the trains.

They stepped outside into a scrum in which flower girls offered them 'luvly violets' and shoeblacks cast scornful looks at their soiled footwear. Eros pointed his arrow towards a cigar emporium; men were unloading carts outside the Trocadero; a bowler-hatted man, whose sandwich board advertised Salutan's distilled water, forced Vickybird briefly off the pavement. Every traffic artery was clogged because of the exhibition, making the walk up Regent Street to Burlington Gardens that much longer. After queuing for ten minutes, Vicky paid the entrance, which was one shilling and three pence each.

They soon spotted the Surrealist Spectre with her uncooked meat, but in the packed rooms, she was not so striking. For one thing, she had to compete with Dali's Aphrodisiac Dinner Jacket, a black tuxedo, located near the entrance, to which were attached dozens of liqueur glasses filled with crème de menthe. Dylan, the most exacting of connoisseurs, slyly reached for one.

'It's a bit early,' muttered his companion terrified they might be seen, though amongst the throng an atmosphere of licence prevailed that was not very English.

Green seemed to be the colour of the moment amongst the spectators, who likewise, through either costume or reputation, dwarfed the Spectre. André Breton, who opened the exhibition, was clad in a green suit and was smoking a green pipe. His wife, standing haughtily beside him, had long green hair.

Delivered in passable English, from a podium set up beside a wire globe containing a female torso called, naturally enough, The Last Voyage of Captain Cook, Breton's opening speech only reinforced Vicky's misgivings. The Frenchman analysed a poem he had written in 1923 and demonstrated that in fact it was a detailed, although obscure prophecy of events that were to occur in 1934. He then described witnessing a street incident in which a painter friend lost an eye. After the event, Breton discovered many one-eyed creatures in the man's earlier work. Was Surrealism, Vicky pondered, occult by nature? Its plan to transform man little different from that proposed by magic?

'I shall have my ears pierced and read the tea leaves,' declared Dylan. 'It's like your man's doodling, I suppose. Life is only waves, wireless waves and electrical vibrations and somehow they connect.'

Vicky lowered his voice: 'Four years before the Great War, Crowley evoked Bartzabel, Spirit of Mars, and used me as the vessel. Employing words I cannot remember saying, though the transcription still exists, I have read it many times, I predicted two wars within the subsequent five years: the storm centre of the first being Turkey; the second, Germany; the result, the destruction of both nations. The prophecy, of course, was horrendously borne out.'

'I'm going to write a poem,' mused Dylan. 'In the first stanza I will get oodles of cash; in the second, a certain young Irishwoman who is beautiful and barmy; in the third the Nobel Prize. I should dash it off right now.'

Instead, he began examining an installation called Object 228, complete with hooks, to one of which somebody had attached a kipper, which was just beginning to stink.

'Do you think the stench is part of the idea?'

'Don't ask me,' replied Vicky. 'I'm a P.I.B. A poor ignorant bastard.'

'Well, it's a bit late for breakfast. This is more like it.' Dylan was referring to a painting of a woman with a real cigarette in her mouth and a small artificial bird glued to her forehead with a piece of sponge, which in fact had been smuggled into the exhibition by an academic painter. The Welshman stole the cigarette and cadged a light from Vicky. 'These super-real fags are terribly good,' he said, 'everyone's wearing bowler hats and floating towards the ceiling.'

Soon he had stumbled on another dodge. Vicky felt a nudge to his elbow. He turned to find the poet proffering him a cup, borrowed from a fur-lined tea set, full of what appeared to be boiled string. 'Weak or strong?' Dylan enquired with exaggerated politeness. This evoked an unexpected response from Vicky. He laughed at such pitch and volume it seemed someone had let a parakeet loose in the room. For a moment, all eyes were on them.

So delighted was Dylan with this wheeze that he approached a tall, heavy-set man a few paces away, who despite the weather was attired in a fedora and long black cloak. The man turned round to reveal a paunchy face made glacial by round pebble glasses. With the excitement of a train spotter clocking a rare engine, Vicky recognised

Wyndham Lewis, founder of Vorticism. 'Molten,' was his retort to Dylan's offer. The poet drifted back as a pale individual, whom Vicky knew from some of the earlier meetings in Boundary Road, began to speak.

'Why does Gascoyne always look as though he grew up in a cellar?' He whispered to Dylan. 'You know what hyacinths are like if you have started them in a cupboard in the dark and forgotten to take them out. One day you open it and find them there – all long white straggly leaves.'

Gascoyne recited from a poem, which spoke of teaching children to sin at the age of five so they would cut out the eyes of their sisters with nail scissors; of angels writing the word Tobacco along the sky; of a girl eating the excrement of dogs and horses.

'May he teach the bats in his belfry better manners,' Dylan commented at the end, though when the poet drifted over the Welshman was all smiles. A grince, that alarming compromise between grin and wince, was the response made by Gascoyne's haunted features, though with Vicky he was distant, reminding the latter he was a comet glowing dully in the trails of Dylan's star.

'The movement's really revving up here now,' said Gascoyne, who seemed to be speaking in French, though the words he used were English. 'You must come and read on the twenty sixth, Dylan. Sam Beckett will be there; he's an Irishman who writes with a razor blade.'

'What a splendid opportunity to unveil my current work in progress,' Dylan agreed. 'It is a short story called "The Phosphorescent Nephew", and bugger me if it's not literary.' He paused and a conspiratorial look wreathed his face as he leaned across to Gascoyne and muttered: 'You know, Davey, Surrealism is a dead horse. That's from Pope Eliot himself.'

'Tom's quite right,' the squeaky voice of the man in the fedora cut in. 'This merging of dream and wakefulness produces nothing but a childish emulsion of life.'

'Hideousness and eccentricity must have a purpose,' Dylan agreed. 'A tomato is not a child's balloon. It's, well ... a tomato!'

'And this is a jellyfish,' added Lewis.

Gascoyne looked hurt. 'I see the revolution will proceed without some. However, we who have angels of anarchy and machines for making clouds cannot let everyone sink into the clutches of the revisionists. Have you seen the De Chiroco, Dylan? He's quite astonishing.'

Grasping the poet by the elbow, he dragged him unresisting into the crowd. Vicky was left with the self-styled Enemy, who breakfasted by popular belief on raw eggs and vodka.

'The intellectual wing of the Communist Party is showing its true colours,' Lewis grunted.

'Oh, I wouldn't say that,' twittered Vicky.

'Wouldn't you, Sir!' Lewis's amazement at being contradicted focused into a curl of one bloodless lip.

'What I see reminds me of Leonardo telling his pupils to stare at the surface of an old cracked wall and paint whatever appeared to them.'

'I see the merely infantile!'

'Of course, there's a black introspection, a delirium posing as ecstasy that is a threat to civilisation and must be checked.'

Lewis examined him as though he were a creature in a zoo. 'Can you see anything black in here? Ah, Osbert, just the man!'

A portly Sitwell with an Edwardian moustache was gliding past. A far more interesting specimen the Enemy had decided. He grabbed him, and conferring loudly, they moved away.

With a sickening lurch, Vicky realised that his jaunt might just be over. Dylan's loud check suit was nowhere to be spotted; instead, strangers ignored him on every side. He felt ashamed of his clipped, tidy hair and forlorn clothes. He looked like an unemployed gamekeeper. Why hadn't he donned the Elizabethan leggings and breeches he had been wont to wear in Steyning, now mothballed in the attic of Boundary Road? He began shuffling towards the exit; the exhibits he passed along the way only serving to confirm the Enemy's judgement.

The Mae West lips pouting over the doorway; the painting of a livid green forest, in which were hidden monstrous figures; even the found objects, such as the metal fish from the Solomon Islands with the tiny skull inside, seemed indeed designed by a child. Moreover, this infant was as cruel as he was capricious. There was the sexual violence implicit in Giacometti's contorted torso, with the wide-open legs and exposed windpipe of the nearly headless corpse. Retrospective Bust of a Woman Devoured by Ants spoke for itself.

To Vicky, who believed art to be a form of applied magic in which it was the burden and privilege of the practioner to glimpse the future in much the way Breton had outlined, these images recalled his visions. This especially applied to an installation near the entrance composed of a twisted, aeroplane-like object with an insect-like shape crawling out of it. Once during trance Vicky had witnessed a plane of entirely new design, bristling with steel, nose-dive into what appeared to be Victoria Station. Burnt and blackened, the pilot had writhed in agony on the platform like an upturned cockroach. The packed room was oppressively stuffy. His woollen jacket made the heat worse as he waded on.

He was brought to a standstill by the pressure of onlookers parting before a craggy faced man bearing a billiard cue. He, in turn, was followed by a figure in a deep-sea diver's suit decorated with green plasticine hands, who was clutching two leashes used to restrain a pair of Borzoi hounds. Vicky hurriedly stepped back for the man in front, was a Scottish poet who had once frequented the meetings in Boundary Road. Vickybird had even less to say to him than he had had to Gascoyne.

The diver ascended the podium and after attempting to deliver his lecture inaudibly from inside the helmet could stand no more. He gestured to the craggy faced man to remove it, radiator cap and all. Unable to loosen the wing nuts by hand, the man commenced using the billiard cue as a lever to work them loose. Meanwhile the diver, with the Borzois' leashes wrapped round his calves, fought to maintain his balance. Eventually, with helmet removed and dogs untangled, the man continued his lecture. Vicky understood, from the heavily accented French, that the speaker was praising a philosophy student who had succeeded in eating a mirror and wardrobe in three years.

After this, there was a little farce.

A diver usually wears absorbent woollen underwear, but because of the heat, the man had remained in his trousers and shirt, which were soaked through with sweat. The speech over, he slumped like a bedraggled eel into an armchair, while his Russian-looking wife dashed out to buy some new clothes. There was a smug expression on the shrewd Catalan face with the trademark moustache. The experience had been as replete with paranoia as any Dali could have wished for.

There was a loud exclamation behind Vicky, the words surprisingly coarse and voice deep considering it was a woman's foot he had squashed. She was stout with rouged cheeks and an incredible bouffant too black for her age, and was not a woman. It had been nearly a quarter of a century since Vicky had seen that face, and make-up could not disguise how in the interim the skin had sagged and grown pitted. He bent his head, mumbled an apology, and shoved his way to the door, now grateful for the haircut that he was sure had prevented recognition. Stepping out into the sunshine was like champagne. Moreover, there, on the highest step, was Dylan, gazing down with delight at a scene unfolding on the pavement.

'The Beast was in there!' Vicky hissed.

'Ah, Vicky, I think you've taken this Super-Real racket a bit too much to heart. There was a clown as well.'

'I mean the man who copied your doodle. He was near the exit dressed as a woman.'

'Great Raven!' cried the Welshman in some alarm.

'He called himself Alys when adopting such a guise in Paris.'

'Can you be sure? After all, it's more than my lifetime since you've seen him.'

'I glimpsed him in the Atlantis Bookshop about two years ago. I had gone in with Runia. He was talking to the manager. I do not think he saw me. We went straight out again.'

'That was the only time?'

'There were also the visits to Steyning. He twice sent his Whore of Babylon. The maid opened the door on the first occasion, had hysterics and handed in her notice that same day.'

'Not a comely doxie then, this Scarlet O'Harlot?'

'She had a ravaged face and drugged eyes. I knew her type well.' He did not add that he had occasionally toyed with such crumbs from the master's table. 'She opened her coat and was naked to the waist. Between withered grey breasts was carved the Mark of the Beast.'

'Bugger me! We should adjourn immediately to somewhere safe like Putney.'

'A week or so later he came himself, but Kathleen, my then wife, waylaid him.'

'What did you do?'

Vicky looked sheepish. 'I ran out the back and hid with a neighbour.'

'An excellent suggestion,' said Dylan, hustling him down the steps.

At the bottom, the now-gloveless Surrealist Spectre was frolicking with a group of pigeons. Either she possessed a curious affinity with animals, or her costume incorporated something of particular delight to them, for one fluttered onto her outstretched hand while another attempted to scale her back. She peered up at their approach.

'There are no more whores in Babylon,' she uttered delphically. The news came as a great relief to Vicky.

'They are conspicuous by their absence,' Dylan agreed, taking her green finger-nailed hand in his own.

III°
Nina

Intimidated by the nearness of the Beast, Vicky suggested they go and eat. 'I always find lunch in London a deliberate lie,' objected Dylan. 'You can be poached out of seven and six for a turnip at Quaglino's or grilled at the Ivy by Abel, who will pretend to recognise you even if you're not in showbiz. Besides, I never eat on an empty stomach. Let's make it drinks.'

This was the last thing of any coherence he was to say for some time, appearing to be in thrall to the Spectre. She, for her part, having dispatched the lovesick pigeons to Trafalgar Square for a later rendezvous, was wafting down Vigo Street, amazing proprietors and customers alike in the cute little galleries that lined the route. Her own utterances careened between the oracular and the bizarre.

'Indeed it was an awesome sight,' she was saying. 'On a beach the conquistadors removed the blindfolds from their captives. They had driven through the night from the city, using up the last of their petrol, so the banker and the priest might witness dawn as the workers do, trudging to the mills. When sunset sleeved the sky with gold, they shot them in the back of the head, but the bullets, displaying considerable sangfroid, melted in the sunbeams and refroze themselves into condors that attacked the town of oak. I fell asleep.'

Dylan, who seemed to find this ending something of an anticlimax, chipped in: 'And on the third day I rose and sold my wife for thirty pieces of Brie and my baby daughter for a hangover.'

Vicky was sure the Welshman could mint a lot more in this vein, but the latter had fallen silent, a wary look on his formerly eager face. Parallel with the Chinese restaurant that marked the turning into Regent Street, they just avoided colliding with two burly men, one of whose brawny arms, bared above the elbow by the rolled up black sleeve, was tattooed with the legend "Mind England's Business". He hissed, the other swore as they spied the Spectre. There you had it, thought Vicky strolling safely on - the poles of the age. However, he could not help wondering if the Spectre and the Blackshirts were not in fact two sides of the same sinister coin.

With the Spectre's veil billowing in the breeze before them, they crossed Regent Street, Vicky barely outdistancing a blue tram that clanged irritably as he scrambled onto the pavement alongside the Galéries Lafayette. He had regained his composure by the time they sauntered past Dunn's, but the trilbies and homburgs glared accusingly, it seemed to him, from the green hat perched on Dylan to his own bare head. He wondered what they made of the owner of a scuffed top hat that had lost its sheen, and shabby eveningwear, the shirt grubby, the trousers fretting into tatters, who stood on the corner of Air Street. There was a tin box in front of him, partially filled with coins, and a sign propped up against this that said, "Hallelujah, I'm a failure." The man had reputedly lost his fortune in the crash but seemed none the worse for it. He grinned and Dylan beamed back.

The Spectre detached a rose from her veil and tossed it to him. Then she abruptly veered off and sailed regally towards the glass doors of the Café Royal. Dylan clenched her arm, his hand restraining where formerly it had caressed.

'The Swiss might be more amenable,' he said in a strangled tone.

'We are expected,' she insisted. Her voice should have been melodious and fluent but was neither.

Dylan skulked after her through the glass doors, engraved with the laurel-bordered N. Vicky brought up the rear. As they entered the marble-lined reception hall, it was Dylan's turn to hang back. With sheepish gestures, he indicated that Vickybird should first penetrate the grillroom. On New Year's Day, still reeling from the toasts at midnight, the rowdy Welshman had scandalised Constant Lambert by rubbing his tongue on a menu and garnishing the composer's entrecote with the resulting gunge. As far as he knew, the Café had not lifted the ban.

No one, however, stopped them, as they turned left into the grillroom, and having chosen a table, slid onto the red plush benches. With Dylan and The Spectre opposite, Vicky lolled beneath the frescoes of nymphs and cupids abandoned to revels discreetly obscured by the fug of rising smoke.

At a table near the window, two pomaded men in toupees, who had not yet heard the Nineties were over, pulled on Turkish cigarettes and sipped Grand Marnier. They were still waiting for Oscar, or more plausibly, Lord Alfred Douglas, a caricature of whom, dressed in what looked like a tea cosy, adorned the wall behind them. Wrinkled and cantankerous, Bosie rarely strayed from his home in Worthing, where, like so many others on the fringes of the time, he flirted with fascism in the form of Major Douglas's theory of Social Credit. Once he had accosted Frank Harris with the line 'Ah! Ancient Pistol', to which the celebrated roué had acidly rejoined 'Well roared, Bottom' - but that was forty years ago.

Much had passed noted Vicky, who had been been a stranger himself to the Café for two decades. The refurbishment carried out piecemeal through the Twenties, which had partitioned the grillroom from the brasserie and destroyed the fabled domino room, had crabbed the place he thought.

Noiselessly, the waiter was upon them.

'My eyes are two piss holes in the sand, my tongue sawdust in a parrot's cage,' declared the son of Swansea, who, emboldened by his apparent reinstatement, ordered Guinness and champagne. The Spectre, very much observed, chose that moment to resume her ramblings.

'The man skims across the blue lake till a wave smashes his breastplate. They only find his shoes; the straps in the cockpit are empty. He has been sucked into the engine and pulverised by the turbines.'

Dylan nodded approvingly. 'I should like very much to be a periwinkle, so that the moon, slicing through the crusts of the waves, would appear to be a beautiful bowl of pea-soup.'

From a stool at the end of the bar, an angular woman was watching them intently. A blue cotton smock, tights and dancer's pumps concealed her bony body; a pink beret, tilted rakishly on her head, marshalled the sweep of her straight brown hair. Vicky glanced at her.

'Does the hank of bone for quim still play its scalding part?' Dylan cut in.

'She reminded me of someone,' Vicky spluttered, turning back.

'What Charlotte-Street Bananas? I always thought you were buttock willing, Vickybird, like those Sodom-hipped creatures to our left.'

'I have never failed a woman sexually,' insisted Vicky. 'I can go on and on.'

'I take your hat off to you.'

Dylan grabbed the Tyrolese from where it perched in a puddle of beer on the table, and doffed it. The Welshman was fascinated and appalled by Oscardom, as he dubbed it, and the question lingered. It was a dangerous subject, but one well suited to the grillroom, with its Edwardian chandeliers, long gilt mirrors and ornate turquoise ceiling. The Spectre was absorbed in balancing some toothpicks on the pepper pot, while the private detective paid to watch the room, sipping coffee near the entrance, was immured to such confessions. It was safe to speak.

'The century was fresh,' Vicky said quietly, 'and I truly believed he was the messiah. He taught me that in adopting such practices I might make myself androgyne, for prior to the Fall, man himself was androgynous and will be again. Besides, it was not just he alone. My readings of Swinburne and Whitman, also led me to that end.'

Dylan found "end" a highly appropriate word. It was the only vice that disgusted him and made him hate his fellow kind. The sin of the boy with the scoutmaster went up like a missile of scum to heaven.

'You have to watch those pundits, particularly the sex ones,' he said instead. 'Wyn Henderson, I don't think you know her, she put me up this Spring in Cornwall, used to stay with Havlick Pelvis a lot. Every morning he crept into her bedroom with a cup of tea. When she had finished it, he gave her another and asked, "Now do you want to make water?" Then he'd give her another cup, hold the chamber pot up enticingly and say, "Surely you must make water now?"'

Dylan had offered him a way out, but Vicky found that once unstoppered, the words poured out like a genie: 'In Algeria we discovered that such nervous excitement and release could be used for the purposes of magic. The Templars learnt this secret from the more esoteric Sufi schools. After that, sex became an instrument of the Work.'

'If you'd offered me a few more francs, dahling, you could have saved yourself all that trouble,' a pantomime-dame voice drawled.

Fleshing out the face, giving back the body its dancer's poise, evicted by two decades of drink and an existence that tumbled from luxury to the hand to mouth with dizzying frequency, Vicky realized he knew the woman in the pink beret now hovering at their table. They had first met at the old Bal Bullier in Paris, a couple of years before the Great War. He had been sitting on the terrace with Crowley and was tipsy after the third pastis his mentor had plied him with, on the grounds that as a pastiche of absinthe it was alcohol-free. Two women had joined them - the one now hovering over them, and the incomparably beautiful Euphemia Lamb, who posed and much else for Augustus John. At that time, only prostitutes wore make up, so Vicky's mistake about these two, with their chalk-white faces, scarlet lips and kohl-rimmed eyes, was forgivable.

'How much did you offer?'

Surprisingly, for such an absent-minded man, he had a good memory for figures. 'Two francs twenty five centimes.'

'I'd give you black velvet,' said Dylan lustily, pulling her down beside him, so he was now wedged delightfully between two women.

'Jade and onyx pearls,' the Spectre added.

The newcomer stared at her with amusement. The private detective, Vicky noticed, was inspecting them like a citizen of Pompeii the volcano.

'Your head is still too big for your body,' said Nina. 'You look like a goat.'

Vicky stiffened. That had really been the upshot of the Beast's curse - a goat not a camel as was commonly believed. Was it just a random image, or did she know? More devastating still, was the thought she traded in print on such tit-bits.

'I saw you last in here,' she said, 'just before the war. The night Crow came in with the butterfly.'

When she roared with laughter, Nina sounded like a man.

'What are you two addled bohemians rambling on about?' demanded Dylan, his pug nose twitching.

'The butterfly was of bronze, dahling, and had been commissioned by the Prefect of the Seine to hide the organ of the winged sphinx that Epstein had carved for Oscar Wilde's memorial at Pére Lachaise,' explained Nina. 'It was simply huge, the organ not the sphinx, my deah. Outraged by this A.C. got into the cemetery one night, stole the butterfly and appeared in the Café the following night wearing it as a codpiece.'

'Tell us about the night Great Raven flew up to the rafters of Big Ben and rung out a Black Mass on the bells,' said Dylan. 'You must have been there, Nina.'

'Oh, I must have been,' she agreed. 'I was everywhere.'

In the cafés of Montparnasse before the war, Nina Hamnett had been as regular a fixture as her friends Picasso and Modigliani. Then, during hostilities, she had gone to the lunches a Russian artist had held in her studio, where the entrance fee of one franc-fifty included a Caporal Bleu and a glass of wine, and eaten with Brancusi and the impoverished Trotsky. She had been the mistress of Gaudier-Brzeska, and had a fund of stories about Gertrude Stein and Hemingway, which she had published three years before in her memoirs Laughing Torso. Her present address was Fitzrovia, of which she was the undisputed queen.

'The more one hears, the more one warms to Great Raven,' chuckled Dylan.

'He is a very dangerous man,' warned Vicky.

'Yes, but erudite and frightfully droll.' Nina countered. 'Do you remember the night he appeared in here in a black cloak decorated with symbols, and wafted slowly through from Regent Street to Glasshouse Street in a sea of flabbergasted silence? He thought he was invisible. No one could convince him the patrons had seen him. "If they saw me, why did nobody speak to me?" he demanded.'

'Perhaps he's peering down at us at this very moment, see through as a nightie.' Dylan said, pinching the Spectre in her side. She gave a little shriek - even her shrieks were dull.

'Only if he has finally attained the Monad that John Dee spoke of,' said Vicky. 'Whoever achieves that is afterwards very rarely beheld by mortal eye.'

Dylan stared at him with frightened eyes. 'Getting technical are you?' he hissed.

'I was always fond of A.C, you know,' said Nina, rummaging in her worn black handbag. 'What others found sinister, I considered intelligence. We were friends. That is why I could never understand his reaction to my book. After all, just think what the papers printed about him in the Twenties. They accused him of drug addiction, spying and cannibalism and he never sued them!'

Nina had exposed the foibles of several celebrities in her book, but not one had decided to sue save Crowley. He had taken exception to a passage that stated he had a temple in Sicily, where he was supposed to practice Black Magic, and from which, one day, a baby was rumoured to have disappeared. Mild besides the allegations the yellow press horrified its readers with, beneath such headlines as a "A Man We'd Like to Hang" or "King of Depravity"; positively anodyne when compared with the lurid description of life at the Abbey of Thelema in Betty May's ghosted autobiography Tiger Woman, which had appeared in 1929.

Crowley, however, had just won a libel case against a bookseller who had advertised his latest novel Moonchild with a mistaken notice that its predecessor, Diary of a Drug Fiend, had been withdrawn from circulation after an attack in the gutter press. The judge had awarded the Beast fifty pound in damages with costs, a fillip to his rapidly depleting income. The most addictive of personalities, he had acquired the worst habit of all – the itch to sue somebody.

'In his top hat and morning coat A.C. looked like an Edwardian fairground magician,' went on Nina. 'When they asked him what the Beast 666 meant, he replied, "Sunlight, you can call me "Little Sunshine".' Hilberry, my counsel, read some of the juicier bits of White Stains. Then they called Betty May who testified about the drinking of blood, drugs and other goings on at Cefalu. Lastly, Hilberry challenged A.C. to make himself invisible.'

'There he isn't again,' squealed Dylan.

'Of course, A.C. lost. However, he declared himself bankrupt. So Constable, my publisher, had to bear the costs.'

'I don't think you know this, Nina,' said Dylan, pouring the last of the Perrier-Jouet into the pool of black liquid and froth at the base of the monogrammed glass. 'Your memoirs had a devastating effect on my career. I was a cub reporter on The South Wales Evening Post when your book came out. I wrote they had banned Laughing Torso. The paper had to grovel. So was nipped in the bud my flirtation with Journelysian.'

'A good job too,' said Vicky, who was beginning to find mixing champagne and Guinness quite elevating.

'No, I didn't know that,' said Nina, with a distracted air. She had just produced from her bag a large prawn and the remains of a Bath Oliver biscuit, both plundered from a party the night before.

'We can do better than that, can't we, Vicky,' exclaimed Dylan. 'You see, everything really is permitted, and health is a red herring. My life consists of miserly carping about a shortage of cash, for I live on the pittance gained by scribbling, and a few rowdy habits and the fret of things not turning out as they should. However, to hell with all that! I am a very happy sort of magpie and do not give a damn. Let's see what's on the board.'

Chalked up beside the bar was the menu of the day: various hors d'oeuvres; a choice of sole and lamb; a dessert called Pôle Nord - all for a not exorbitant four shillings and sixpence.

'That prawn's really filled me up. I'll have a bite of yours.'

'Vicky can stand us. It's a French letter day!'

'Nobody ever offers me anything to eat,' said Nina choking back a sob. 'They buy me drinks but nothing to eat.'

Vicky, who was a generous man as well as the possessor of five pounds, which Runia had inserted in his wallet in order to pay the printers of The Comment Treasury, clucked sympathetically and called the waiter. The women ordered fish, the men lamb, and Dylan, who was partial to sweets, a bottle of Veuve Cliquot.

'This is very kind of you, Victor,' said Nina. 'Many people ask after you, you know. To them you are "the poet". That is what I called you in Laughing Torso. It's the bit about Ione that really gets them.'

The shadow that crossed Vickybird's face was unconnected with those dancing on the bar, cast by the flames from the chafing dishes, or with any other that obscured the submarine illumination of the grillroom. Ione de Forrest, whose real name was Joan Hayes, had made something of a name for herself as a dancer before joining Crowley's circle. She had an exquisite face of the Russian ballet type, oval with beautifully defined eyebrows. Her body was like that of a child of twelve.

'I came upon them once, you know,' Nina went on in hushed tones, 'in that flat in Victoria Street. She was standing behind A.C. as he sat at a table. She was stroking his hair, or rather that phallic quiff that was all that remained of it, saying "Aleister" repeatedly. Odd if you think about it. None of us used his first name: it was always "A.C." - or "Crow" if you were really intimate.'

'We were all in his sway, even you, Nina.' Vicky said, striving to conceal his shock, but Dylan noticed.

'Vickybird's gone as white as Christmas!' he barked, the fork with which had skewered a roll mop from one of the plates of hors d'oeuvres the waiter was setting down, suspended in mid-air.

'I'm not surprised. Finding Ione dead was the most ghastly thing that ever happened to me. Can you bear it, Victor? Will you let me speak?' Nina did not wait for a reply. 'I had seen her the day before and she had seemed quite put down. She told me she was going away for a long time and I should come back the following morning when she would give me some clothes. I was thrilled because I was down to my last dress. The next day I went to her studio. Outside, pinned on the door, was an envelope with a key in it. I opened the door and inside was a large red curtain. I hesitated for a moment, simply terrified. I pulled it aside and found her lying on the sofa with a mother-o'-pearl revolver and her slippers beside her on the floor. Her face was white and eyes half-closed. She had placed the revolver to her chest and shot herself through heart and lungs.'

'Ione was a temperamental girl,' Vicky said. 'The rituals and the drugs had unbalanced her.'

The others were looking at him expectantly, yet how, in those cheerful surroundings, could he go on to relate that two days before Ione's suicide Crowley had evoked the Spirit of Mars and used him as the vessel. The Beast had overlooked the banishing ritual, and for seventy-two hours, Vicky had felt as though he were stuck in a tiny room with a maniac. Vickybird was sure it had been deliberate. Crowley had been jealous of Ione and her hold on him. The Beast could never stand a rival. She had been in low spirits when he went to her. He had not felt like staying. "If you go out of that door," she had screamed, "I shall kill myself." "All right," he had answered, "kill yourself." No one had discovered his crime, yet even a quarter of a century later, he could not bring himself to confess to that murder by the word.

'She always seemed to have a secret that was a kind of burden to her,' prompted Nina. 'I mean she left you, married that man Merton, and then came back to you. I never understood it.'

Nina's eyes brimmed with enquiry, but from Vicky she would never receive an answer. By nature he was a garrulous man, and though experience had taught him that gossiping inspired contempt, it was not this that stayed his tongue, but the truth itself – so pathetic, heartrending and perverse.

'The worst thing was that I did not break with A.C. immediately afterwards,' he said. 'I actually believed him when he told me she was Lilith and in her moved the treacherous humours of the moon.'

'She was Luna during the Rites at the Caxton Hall,' said Nina. 'She wore a flowing white robe with a fillet of silver leaves around her head. She was stiff, though, her voice faint and performance wooden. It was you who were the star, Victor deah, wheeling round and round like a dervish, then suddenly collapsing and shooting across the floor like an unfurling sail.'

Dylan peered at him with interest. 'I never fancied you as a Nijinsky.'

'Oh, it was just something I made up,' answered Vicky, who was modest to the point of masochism. 'I had watched such dances in Algeria. Once or twice, the spirit was not with me, but the other times I danced down the God and became Mars manifest in London - four years early, if you like. The mescal, of course, played its part.'

'That was the strange drug we were all using,' observed Nina.

'Dancing! Drugs! What next?' Dylan gleefully rubbed his hands together.

'Mescal gives the fastest access of anything I know to the astral. We mixed it with punch before the performance and passed it around the audience. Then we'd drink some ourselves.'

'He never offered me any,' said Nina, 'but I can remember him giving it to a rich marmalade manufacturer, who had come to study magic. You know the type, more money than sense. He was stone deaf, so every now and then A.C. would write on a piece of paper, "What are your impressions?" and the jam magnate wrote, much to A.C.'s disgust, "I see coloured patterns like the tiles in the V and A."'

She had gained the interest of the Spectre who wanted to know where she could get some.

'Mescal is extracted from a Central American cactus,' said Vicky dubiously. 'I would be surprised if you could find any in London in these more sober days.'

'A pity,' sighed Dylan. 'I also need something to alter the course of the tiny boat that circles the Anglesey of my egotism; lotuses that will make me cease to care if "peninsula" or "drome" is the lovelier word.'

'You need no such thing,' Vicky was stern.

'But in a way I do want to discard all I've ever scribbled and set off again, vibrating with new awe, free of my dismal concerns and the Black Death that is sophistication. I long for the rites of passage of the sky. I want to believe that paradise is being and inferno a region of myself I can scorch with its own flame.'

'But you have such a distinct voice and a growing public.'

'I don't care a damn for an audience or success, Vicky.'

'You sound just like 'Gus John,' said Nina. 'He always says the "Public" is the concern of the theatrical producer and the whore - not the artist.'

'I suppose it's nice to have something appreciated for the reasons one wrote it by someone not influenced by the bitchy schools and the smart things one doesn't want to understand like Relativity and Krishnamurti. However, in the end, celebrity is a con, cabals abound, and the only Cable Wallah a relatively truthful person like me can join is one plugged directly into the mains. Electrify the lot of them, that's the motto.'

So saying he took a hearty swipe at the plate of lamb that had appeared upon the table. Nina and the Spectre, however, were just picking at their fish.

'The food's very good,' said the former, embarrassed by her lack of appetite, 'but the place isn't what it was. Before the refurbishment, it was a slice of Paris battened down in Piccadilly with sawdust on the floor, dominoes, and pen and paper available if the mood took you to write or sketch. It was a real bastion against that dreadful Anglo-Saxon hatred of the artist. When 'Gus John came in, my deahs, the students from the Slade would stand in silent homage. And do you know, after the dinner given for Rodin, the horse was unyoked from his four-wheeler? A mob of fellows bore him down Regent Street hollering his name all the way.'

A gaunt individual came up to the table and presented them with a grubby visiting card inscribed with his name and the words "Jobbing Poet, Funerals Attended."

'I'll do yours, if you do mine,' Dylan offered affably, his chin smeared with mint and cream. The man drifted dourly off in the direction of the faded Nineties aesthetes, who looked as though they might require his services at any moment.

'Well, Crosland's still here,' Dylan went on, 'and I hear Lennox Pawle can be found in the brasserie pushing wax matches into his cheeks and setting them alight.'

'The clowns are always the last to leave the circus,' agreed Nina. 'But you hardly ever see 'Gus John, nor anymore of Orage, genially presiding over his "New Agers".'

'You drop more names than Abel at the Ivy,' complained Dylan. 'Who's next for a walk-on? Alberic Morphine?'

Nina ignored this. 'Orage was always looking for a master,' she said. 'He even flirted with A.C. for a while.'

'Orage was a kind and honest man,' put in Dylan, 'but to my mind almost completely lacking in taste. It was quantity not quality when he ran the New English Weekly. He didn't pay, and the standard was so low it was no great shakes to be accepted.'

'You're right, dahling, New Age was so much better,' said Nina. 'But after the war he got in thick with that Russian fellow, spent years in America and grew completely out of touch. What is it about such men that make them follow someone when they should jolly well sort out their lives for themselves? You heard about, Mudd, I suppose, Vicky? They found him in Guernsey Harbour a couple of years back. His pockets were stuffed with pebbles and he was still wearing bicycle clips – ludicrous to the last.'

Vicky was not surprised by the squalid death of the gangling youth who had spanielled after him carrying esoteric tomes to meetings of the Pan Society. Then the god himself had appeared, in the person of Aleister Crowley, complete with rings, scent and an air of having penetrated not just exotic countries but the very mysteries themselves. Mudd was lost. His parents had forced him to abjure the Beast, but his studies were devastated, and gaining a miserable degree, he had found a post in South Africa, where he had gone in order to get the bug out of his system – unsuccessfully, Vicky with a shudder realised now.

'A.C. was worse than horse for him,' continued Nina. 'I used to see him on the terrace of La Rotonde in the early Twenties. He looked so shabby and forlorn I would invite him for coffee, though most of the time I was down to my last few sous meself. Leah, the skeletal Whore of Babylon, was sometimes with him. They got married, I believe. A.C. had dumped them both after being thrown out of Sicily.'

Vicky pondered the union, consecrated in the shadow of the Beast, of the squat Mudd and the soiled creature he had contemplated with horror on his doorstep at Steyning. It was true. Crowley was like a drug. He wondered if there was a cure.

Dessert arrived: a semi-fluid ice cased in harder ice cream shaped like a bird resting on rocks. The conversation seemed to have frozen into a silence so extended that Dylan felt compelled to puncture it:

> "There was a bloody chaffinch
> Flew up a bloody chine
> Came a bloody thunderstorm
> Which knocked the bugger for nine."

'I think that's awfully good; I say it about twice a day and laugh and laugh. Wyn taught it me in Cornwall.'

Wyn Henderson was a boozy journalist and publisher who had counted Crowley amongst her authors. Dylan had heard a lot about the Beast already in Polgigga that April.

No one wanted mazagram, a coffee and milk concoction that was a speciality of the Café, mainly because Vicky had run out of cigarettes. With champagne, the bill came to just under the two pounds he made it up to with the tip.

As they were walking out the private detective rose and with a relieved air escorted them to the exit. He was a thickset man with a ruddy face, mutton chop sideboards and piggy eyes that sized up the Welshman from his bonnet of unruly curls to the tips of his scuffed shoes. Suede had recently shaken off its "pansy" overtones but was still highly suspect as far as he was concerned.

'I'm glad you didn't feel the need to provide anyone with garnish, Mr. Thomas,' he chuckled.

Dylan wheeled unsteadily round and stuck out his chin. 'Bewilder 'em,' he boomed.

IV°
Life No. 13

Beneath a genial sky, London was enjoying a typical early summer afternoon. The Exhibition of Surrealism had halted the traffic around Piccadilly and attracted fifteen hundred spectators. This was out of a daytime population of some seven million. Most were more bemused than scandalised by the fact that the avant-garde now accommodated fur-covered tea sets and levitating men wearing the same bowler hats that thousands of them were longingly eyeing on the hat stands of their offices at that very moment. Soon they could put them on and commute to the smug and leafy arbour of the suburbs.

At newsstands, vendors were barking out the names of the three Evening papers on sale. The Standard was first tempting its readers with the front-page adverts, then informing them that Neville Chamberlain had pulled a four-year-old boy out of the pond in St. James's Park the previous afternoon. Alongside this reassuring testament to the Chancellor's valour was the alarming report of a plague of adders in the West Country. Yet, though the more diligent reader might stumble on a few lines detailing the new threats Japan was making against China, he would not find a word about Spain. Within a month, the peninsula would erupt into a civil war. Nor was there any mention of Herr Hitler, who was presumably doing his utmost to safeguard the interests of the British Empire even as he marched into the Rhineland. Moreover, disappointingly, there was not an iota about Aleister Crowley, that old staple of the yellow press, who had more or less dropped out of sight since being prosecuted for the theft of Betty May's letters in 1935.

The Beast, in fact, was at that very moment in a hotel room not a mile from Oxford Circus. Having discarded the wig, dress and stockings in which he had welcomed surrealism, he was plying the obese thighs of a married woman of forty-two with "tantric" caresses. These, along with Elixir of Life pills partially composed of the masseuse's semen, constituted "Amrita", a treatment designed to remedy her failure to attract - the cost a guinea a session. Blissfully unaware of these exertions, Victor Neuburg sailed towards his old master like the Titanic to its iceberg.

Vicky was relieved Nina had not decided to loop her arm through his in the way the Spectre had commandeered Dylan's. He strolled on unencumbered, beneath the awnings of shops whose windows displayed cashmere shawls and leather travelling cases, until the couple in front swayed to a halt before Salmon and Gluckstein's. Dylan detached himself from the Spectre, and taking Vicky by the arm marched him smartly into the tobacconist's.

'Are you rolling in it temporarily?' chirped the poet. "Would you like to lend me some money, a pound or at the very most, two pounds?'

A frown harried Vicky's features, prompted by having to think of money, which he found distasteful, not by the refusal that Dylan now anticipated. The Welshman was dreaming of wads of cash, which he would squander on quim, champagne, and doctors, champagne again, and a very vague Irish woman he had met two months before. Vicky removed his wallet and fished out a ten-shilling note, noticing, as he did so, that Dylan was hatless.

'You must have left it in the Café Royal,' he said reproachfully.

Dylan ran a hand through his red-tinged locks and decided a diversion was in order. 'That's a new way of getting ill,' he said, jabbing in the direction of one of the pouches on the shelves. 'You buy an ounce of Navy Plug, a little machine for making roll-ups and a packet of cigarette papers. The result is a taxi-driver's glove.'

Brandishing his ten-bob note, he bought twenty Woodbines from the ashen-faced assistant behind the counter. Vicky, in the meantime, gazed at the shelves, relishing as he always did the neat rows of packets with their evocative designs: the green Three Castles with the sailor boy on a jetty; the pink-bordered Passing Clouds with the puffing cavalier. In the end, he settled on a packet of Gold Flake.

'You know I have to spend weeks after these regular short trips to the Capital Punishment sending abject telegrams of apology,' said Dylan as they made their way out. 'I arrange my itinerary in the nicest way. I resolve to discuss Saint Jerome with Pope Eliot and twitter on about George Eliot with Pamela Johnson. Then, when I come to town, all these good intentions are scattered in a tornado of booze, leaving limbs and coloured shirts spinning in the gusts. I spend days searching for the pub where I mislaid a shoe. Life No.13 sucks me into clouds of women, drink, a great expanse of talk and nothing left for work. Then I return to Swansea, with Life No. 13's bile and self-loathing.'

Ahead, now arm-in-arm, Nina and the Spectre swayed to a stop and peered into a large display window. The Spectre turned to them, rigged like a galleon, waiting for Dylan to reboard.

'You know, Vicky, I met someone in April,' confided the latter in hushed tones. 'She is two months younger than I, has an ocean of golden hair, blue eyes, a dancer's legs, is messy and fey and does not nag. I am adrift with desire and poverty.'

The women were standing before a window lined with evening gowns and summer frocks, which had, in deference to the prevailing fashion, shelf-shoulders arranged in several tiers. With the men now in tow, they shuffled further along and were arrested at the next window by "Guardee" overcoats, which boasted braided epaulettes, cord shoulder straps, and rows of gleaming metal buttons. Lastly, they came upon a display of beach dress. Floppy beach-pyjamas were now passé: instead tailored sailor trousers and vests, with slim hips and high waists, jostled for their custom. Dylan began to sing "Bobby Shaftoe" in a pleasing baritone.

Vicky glanced at his watch and considered his options. It was well past four. The day was cooling and a light breeze restored in him an alertness that drink and the Café had dulled. In a few minutes, they would reach Oxford Circus. There he could scuttle into the underground and journey home to Runia's reproaches. The prospect was unappealing, but his money was almost gone as was his enthusiasm for an evening spent drinking in such volatile and thirsty company. Nina chose that moment to coil her bony arm through his. Vicky blanched but he should not have worried. Nina, who had been the mistress of many men and had even slept with Crowley on one occasion, now reserved her affections exclusively for boxers and sailors - anyone, in fact, whose stamina outmatched their intellect.

'Dahling, you shall come to the Fitzroy Tavern,' she commanded.

'No, the Fitzroy and the Wheatsheaf are out of bounds,' barked Dylan from behind. 'I'm sick of hacks rambling on about the novels they'll never write and music hall comedians with bible-glum faces. There used to be a lovely pub in Hackney until an invasion of the beards. I think the Anchor's spruce these days, and the one Younger's house in Queensway has no murders until about eight-thirty. Let's go there.'

'But I've got a tab at Pop's!' protested Nina.

In the window of Hamley's, a large sign was inviting children to build their own Maginot Line. On show, Vicky noted, was a cross-section of tiered dugouts with little men in them performing a variety of duties. An advance patrol was crawling through fields, meeting with heavy fire in the form of cotton wool that puffed across the landscape.

There was a sequence of explosions behind Vicky. He reeled round. Bricks, coping stones, furniture and flakes of glass, from which a thin plume of blue smoke was spiralling, were strewn in heaps down Regent Street. The windows of the Galleries Lafayette had all been blown out. Another store had thrown its entire front onto the pavement. Water fizzed from holes made by flying glass in the hoses snaking down the street.

Dylan was to one side, propping him up, while on the other was Nina. They conferred over his slumped head for a moment, then hustled him across the road, and, with the Spectre in tow, boarded an open-roofed number nine on its way to the British Museum. They propelled Vicky up the stairs that projected out like a concertina at the back. At the front of the deck, a party of schoolchildren in starched uniforms and their matronly teacher accompanied their entrance with astonished giggles and a sharp "Be quiet!"

'What's up, Vicky?' demanded Dylan as he placed a Woodbine between Vicky's lips and lit it, before lighting his own.

'Mars,' murmured Vicky too dazed for concealment. 'Once evoked, you see, he can always come back.'

'That's what you meant when you told me magic works?'

Vicky agreed, savouring the late sunlight glistening on windows restored to their former wholeness and a street whose only heap was a tramp sleeping it off in the staff doorway of Peter Robinson's.

'Once, in a hotel room in Paris, I saw an immense form materialize before me which I believed to be Jupiter. However, I do not know to this day if the form possessed an objective existence outside myself or if it was a product of my fancy. Perhaps in the end it's impossible to know, but yes, magic works.'

'When I first knew A.C.,' Nina's tone was low and husky, 'he asked me to paint four panels representing the elements. While I was painting Fire, the Fire Element apparently escaped, and three fires started in mysterious ways in the studio on the same day. And another time, you remember, Vicky dahling, when we were dancing in a circle at 124?'

'Ah, the stranger,' sighed Vicky.

'We were going round the altar with linked hands and faces turned outwards,' Nina went on. 'The temple was dimly lit and heavy with incense. Somehow, the circle was broken. We kept on dancing. Then we became aware of the presence of a stranger. I counted the men present and found there was one too many. Then someone switched on the light.'

'That was me,' said Vicky. 'I was always looking for something that would verify the experience, you see. There was no stranger to be seen.'

Hemmed in by taxis and Harrod's delivery vans the bus crawled along Oxford Street. Banners, flying from flagpoles that jutted from the windows of stores along their route, advertised a school of English, "Doral's" permanent wave and passport photos. The bemused conductor collected the fares, which Vicky paid, just as the bus pulled up before a restaurant called "This is the Plaice". The others helped Vickybird down the stairs and onto the pavement.

A few steps down this side street erased the crowds of milling shoppers and the smug department stores. In their place were strollers more confident of their territory - a district of patisseries and delicatessens, from which wafted the smell of baguettes, olive oil and wurst. They were entering Fitzrovia, the closest thing to a Latin Quarter London ever had.

Of London's bohemias, the others being Hampstead and Chelsea, Fitzrovia was the poorest. It suited the aspirant, the camp follower, and any of the vanguard that fashion had not blessed with respectability nor showered with cash such as Wyndham Lewis who had a studio in Percy Street. There were eccentrics too, like the self-styled King of Redonda, with his title-giving ceremonies, or the poet Count Geoffrey de Montalk, son of a New Zealand milkman, who claimed to be the rightful King of Poland and affected a green cloak, sword and scabbard, and shoulder-length hair. In essence, Fitzrovia would always be the home of the pretender, who wondered why he was still in the baggage train as he borrowed and drank.

Nina, whose own work was suffering a serious eclipse for all the usual reasons, was the bush telegraph of the area as well as its principal giver of nicknames. She had christened the dowdy, down-at-heel pub they were passing 'The Burglar's Rest' because she had once found a jemmy on the bar-billiard table. Incidents from her anecdotal life littered the area, as she proceeded to illustrate:

'If we had come up from Fitzroy Square, dahlings, we would have passed the house where I lost my virginity. Do you know Rimbaud and Verlaine occupied the same digs when they were in London?'

'Bugger me!' said Dylan.

'When I told Sickert, he said they should put a blue plaque up for me at the front, and one for the Frenchies at the back!'

At the end of Rathbone Place, past the mock-tudor beams of the Wheatsheaf, lay a small unmarked square. On the corner, beside the Scala Cinema, two racks bristled with newspapers that catered to the homesickness of the large foreign community: Figaro bemoaned the general strike in France; Der Welt Spiegel crowed over the unopposed remilitarization of the Rhineland. Each had a section mysteriously cut out - news of the latest escapades of the King and Wallis Simpson.

The premises within doubled as a café. They could have drunk at the 'Jubilee', a drinking club that lay over the road, but Nina had over-extended a tab based on a large mural she was supposed to be designing, which had yet to see paint set to plaster. They entered the café, which was called Buhler's.

Books lined the interior, all of them foreign, and the floor was taken up by tables and elegant high-backed chairs only one of which was in use. The occupant, a large black gentleman, dressed in the tiger-skin robes and feathered headdress of a Zulu chieftain, was being served with tea and a tray of cakes by a short woman whose grey hair was tied back into a bun. After fussing over her customer a few moments longer than was necessary, she came over to the table they had collapsed around. She favoured Nina with a smile, but grew prim as, from behind gold-rimmed spectacles, her eyes took in the frayed cuffs of Vicky's jacket, the veil and roses of the Spectre, and lastly Dylan's leer.

'I don't serve him,' she said. 'Last time he tries to bite postman.'

Dylan blushed like a schoolboy.

'Oh dahling, how dreadful,' cooed Nina. 'Just three Viennese coffees, then.'

A great fan, Madame Buhler, the eponymous proprietress, scurried off.

'I've got a filly for you Saturday, Miss Nina,' the black man boomed across the room.

'Quid's in, Prince Monolulu,' shouted Nina.

After the coffee arrived, Vicky surreptitiously offered Dylan a sip, but the latter haughtily insisted that he let no liquid pass his lips, which did not contain alcohol. When the cuckoo clock on the wall struck half past five, he grew frantic to leave. Vicky settled the bill, and with Bertorelli's, famed for the cheapness of its spaghetti, to their left, they crossed the square diagonally, approaching a red-bricked, Victorian pub, whose frosted-glass doors opened at Dylan's shove. The Fitzroy Tavern was the Clapham Junction of Fitzrovia, as Augustus John had put it, with the rider that eventually everyone must pass through it.

Small bags of coins festooned the ceiling, which were intended to send the poorer children of the quarter to the seaside. The instigator of this charity, a large man with a lined, genial face, waxed moustaches and a perfectly groomed imperial beard, greeted them from behind the bar.

'Make mine a double gin, Pop,' said Nina, 'and whatever the rest of them want. On the tab, I'm afraid.'

Such was the infrequency of Nina ordering a round, inviting her being as mandatory as last orders, that 'Pop' Kleinfield, the burly Russian proprietor, hesitated a moment longer than was necessary.

'Pint of Toby's!'

'Glass of red wine!'

'Crème de menthe!' demanded the voices, mellifluous, shrill, and flat, of the others.

Once served, they took a table beneath one of several First World War recruiting poster that lined the walls. From this vantage, they observed the mix of regulars and what Dylan in a disgusted tone called "day trippers", though he was one himself. These occupied the tables and barstools over the next forty minutes or put pennies in the electric pianola, a magnificent instrument adorned with lights on the front and pale pink shades trimmed with glass beads. There were a few faded women, once models, now crones; a pair of Music Hall comedians, their faces with the greasepaint removed, curiously shiny, who sat glumly hunched at a table near them. There were two toffee-voiced Oxford undergraduates, sporting boaters, plus-fours and co-respondent's shoes, desperate to pad off to the illicit delights they knew lay somewhere in the vicinity.

Just after six Augustus John appeared. Nina, who had followed him in silent adoration down the King's Road some thirty years before, and then, on meeting, had discovered an indissoluble bond in the fact they were both from Tenby and had shared the same dancing-and-German teacher, hailed him with enthusiasm. To the star struck Vicky the painter's entrance was like the splash of a wave - he was in the swim again. In the gilded epoch before the war, he had often seen John and had sat at his table on one occasion. With his long hair, brass earrings and black polo neck the painter had been swashbuckling and magnificent as he excited the coterie of nymphs who surrounded him with laughter and the occasional caress. Two decades on, the earrings were of gold, and Augustus, attired in a Panama hat and double-breasted white suit with a brightly coloured bandana round his neck, had grown a paunch and his red hair was flecked with grey.

'I went to that utterly insane exhibition, dahling. Met this lot at the Café,' explained Nina.

Cultivating a slightly muzzy air, Augustus passed over Vicky's beaming countenance without a flicker. Falling on Dylan and the Spectre, his grey-green eyes registered surprise and a frown harried the lines.

'No time for those Super-realists and their nursery art,' huffed the painter, 'though Bert Read kept on at me to go. What did you make of it, Dylan?'

'It convinced me that my own well-balanced leek can never be a pal of the French mandrake forever shrieking itself to a loud and undignified death with roots of boiled string.'

'Humph!' exclaimed Augustus, little the wiser, a fact unconnected with his deafness. 'Looks like you need to wet your Kâri.' (This was Romany and meant penis). 'Same again, I suppose, Nina, and you, Sir?' to Vicky, 'Another glass of wine?' He wheeled round and peered at the Spectre with melodramatic intensity. 'A crème de menthe as always, Delia?'

A collective gasp was prompted by the discovery they knew each other.

'Why is it that with every woman I have ever met, King John got there first?' Dylan muttered as Augustus sauntered over to the bar.

'I sat for him,' the Spectre said, seeming to have come down to earth with a bump now she was unmasked.

'On him more like,' murmured Dylan in a whisper only audible to Vicky.

Returning with the drinks, the painter was hailed by one of the music hall comedians.

'Hello, Augustus,' said the veteran. 'You're growing old.'

'I'll never catch up with you, Barry,' replied the painter.

It was a little early for his usual double dark rum and whisky but the painter had bought one nonetheless. He began sipping it, looking from the Spectre to Dylan in a way Vicky deciphered as distinctly hostile. 'Looks like you're set to make a night of it,' he commented,

'Here for the duration,' Dylan, who had drunk over half of the second pint, agreed.

'The difference between a scribbler and a painter is that the latter depends so much upon the sky, at least in a country like this which boasts only weather, never a climate,' Augustus reflected. 'If a painter burns the candle, it may mean getting up late next day and missing a priceless ray. The poet does not have that problem. He can get up any time he pleases. A fountain pen, an exercise book and a packet of fags are all he needs for a studio.'

'If you took up Surrealism, Augustus,' replied Dylan, 'you could dispense with the weather entirely.'

A slight redness sallied up the painter's cheeks. Not so inadvertently, perhaps, the Welshman had hit the mark. Augustus had the adoration of society hostesses; his ménage at Alderney with the enigmatic Dorelia; the services of models such as Caitlin Macnamara, whom he had been sketching that very morning at a house in Hampshire. He was a standard celebrity fêted on playing cards, yet was conscious of trawling the shallows - of the current being elsewhere. His eyes expanded like sea anemones as he appraised Dylan.

'You always serve to confirm for me two truths I have stumbled on in my career. The first is that the authentic derives from staying a kid as long as possible; the second is that loafing around often yields more fruit than industry!'

Dylan was saved from having to reply by the noisy entrance of the African gentleman they had seen at Madame Buhler's. He had changed into a multi-coloured satin jacket covered with horseshoes, four-leaf clovers and winning posts. 'I've got a horse, I've got a horse,' he bellowed. An owlish figure, still enveloped in the black cloak and fedora he had been wearing earlier in the day, followed him. Basilisk-like, his eyes glinted down at them through the horn-rimmed spectacles.

'I have seen the future,' he declared grandiloquently, 'and it is a kindergarten!'

'Yes, of course, it is, Wyndham,' agreed Augustus, who after solicitously helping his myopic friend onto a chair, went over to the bar and returned with refills for them all and a second crème de menthe intended for Lewis. There was a pained expression on the latter's face, induced by his just having bumped into an important art critic in Charlotte Street.

'I put out my hand,' he explained, 'and something got hold of it, something very slimy. I looked down, and, Gus, it was a marine growth. I was really frightened, I had to get my hand away from its suckers and was very relieved to be able to manage it.'

After this cheerful exercise in paranoia, Augustus decided to introduce Lewis to the one member of the company he did not know, but hesitated, at something of a loss. Nina came to his rescue.

'This is Victor Neuburg, dahling.'

'Actually, we have been introduced before,' Vickybird reminded the painter in a timid voice. 'When Marinetti performed at Madame Strindberg's.'

Vicky was referring to The Cave of the Golden Calf, which had stood just round the corner from the Café Royal. On the night in question the Italian artist, complete with gold chains, diamond rings and gleaming white teeth, had loudly declaimed his Futurist manifesto, vigorously accompanied by drums and ear-splitting noises from his band.

'It was Marinetti who put Mussolini up to Fascism,' declared Lewis in his squeaky voice. 'They ran neck and neck for a bit, but Mussolini was the better politician. Still, that dreadful wop brought off a Futurist putsch in London.'

'What a racket!' groaned Augustus. 'It still gives me a headache to think about it. And if I consider that walking hell-bitch Frieda Strindberg I might have a seizure.'

'She was trying to build up a palace of all the Arts,' added Lewis, 'with stale patchouli, sawdust and champagne.'

'I cannot say I recall our meeting,' Augustus went on.

Vicky told him with whom he had been.

'Ah, you orbited that dark star, did you? Well, I would not go so far as to say any friend of his is a friend of mine, but it is a pleasure to meet you again. Some find Crow's lurid reputation intoxicating, but I have never been in awe of him. Nevertheless, he is the horse's mouth about magic, white or black, and once he stops playing the mage, can be good company. The Beast possesses a lot more than the wares of a charlatan, but lacks discrimination.'

'The times I've run into him made me realise a startling truth,' said Lewis. The others looked at him expectantly. 'The Beast is a woman!' Happy to have dropped this bombshell, the Bombardier smirked.

'He certainly likes dressing up as one,' said Dylan.

'And assuming the passive role,' added Vicky unprompted.

This inside information attracted everyone's interest. Vickybird blushed. Lewis was the first to break a silence verging on the awkward.

'Even his bosomy physique is feminine. He is a relic of the Purple Years: the vengeance of Oscar personified. He should have joined forces with Lawrence when he came out with all that baloney about blood and sun.'

'Ah Lawrence,' sighed Dylan. 'He ranted on about the gods, and as far as his tuberculosis permitted, tried to lead a pagan life. However, the more one relishes sex and the sun, the less hope in hell one has of writing. A writer is born in a darkened room. His imagination gives the shadows form. A creed like paganism, which flaunts the life of the body and reconciles man to his condition, is of no damned use to him. Personally, I have no need of pine forests and cacti. I am not even a country dweller. I'd rather contemplate the flinty Welsh sky than sunshine.'

'England's all right, I suppose,' sighed Lewis, 'but what's the use of it being an island, if it's not a volcanic one. You will find out Dylan. You are very much the young lion now, but when the bubbly and the cheers are exhausted, you will slink back to Wales cursing the grinning barbarians who dwell by the Thames. What was that dream you had, Augustus?'

'Dream? Oh yes, I remember. I was conversing with a society woman of scintillating brilliance and wit,' explained the painter with a guffaw. 'But all I could recall when waking was her saying, "Britannia's hard on the lions!"'

Lewis, whose own moment of fame, inspired by the appearance of Blast, had been blown to smithereens by the war, nodded vehemently.

Finding all this a trifle indulgent, Augustus nudged them magisterially back to Lawrence: 'Lady Cynthia Asquith, whose portrait I was painting, brought him round one day to my studio. She wanted me to paint the writer and I was interested. However, Lawrence protested that he was too ugly. I never did insist on an Adonis for a model. After all, I have sketched Crowley, and done your portrait, Dylan.'

'A masterpiece in miniature,' waxed Lewis.

Ignoring this applause, the painter continued: 'That night Lady Cynthia treated us to a box at the opera. On leaving, Lawrence announced that he had the urge to howl like a dog. I never saw him again, but I went to the show of his paintings in Maddox Street. Daubs and botches, thought I, but the police, were much more taken with them and apart from Lawrence's work, carried off a number of designs by Blake as well!'

Raising his pint, Dylan leaned forward and hissed: 'I am in the path of Blake, but so far behind that only the wind of his wings catches me.'

The painters looked at him then, as if of one accord, gazed at the Spectre. If they had been gourmets and women dishes, Lewis had sampled almost as many recipes as his friend. The swathe he had cut through society hostesses and models had not been as wide, nor as deep but mixed in similar proportion plenitude and the ludicrous. Famously, for instance, he had once been copulating with his landlady's daughter on the floor of a hallway when the post was delivered and a shower of letters cascaded onto his bare behind. Spread before them now, the upper slopes of the Spectre's bust jutted out of her disarrayed dress. In contrast to the flatness of her personality, her breasts were voluminous, ripe and eloquent. Both men's eyes glinted in appreciation. Dylan chose that moment to howl like a dog.

'Aping Lawrence, eh!' said Lewis.

'More likely dogging him,' said Augustus with a guffaw.

Nina tittered dutifully.

'I read about you today, Wyndham, in the Telegraph,' said the painter, when both howling and laughter had subsided. 'They reviewed your new book quite favourably.'

'My peace pamphlet, you mean.' Lewis was referring to his polemic *Left Wings over Europe*. 'Someone had to take a stand against the dreadful Hitler Complex that infects this country.'

'But Germany is an ogre,' objected Vicky, emboldened by the wine. 'The Nazis will devour us all.'

'Gobbling Goebbels,' put in Dylan.

'Why ever should the Germans wish to bomb Great Britain? It is only folly, or malice,' said Lewis, with a warning glance at Vicky, 'to think otherwise. Look what Hitler has done. He's tamed the Press, executed Bolsheviks, prevented Jews from lining their pockets with gold. Outrageous! He is apt to seize Danzig, an awfully cute city on the Baltic. Abominable! I am prepared to prophesy that when the rest of the world has spurned England, Adolph will be there – nobly helping her.'

'Hitler is the harbinger of a new Dark Age!' said Vicky.

Lewis groaned: 'Look around! Do you see Periclean Athens?'

An old woman had taken her teeth out and was polishing them in Guinness on the table nearest to the pianola, which was being assiduously fed with coins by a florid individual with several chins. This was Constant Lambert, whose New Year dinner Dylan had so memorably garnished. The composer's presence explained why the Welshman had dragged the hat and veil from the Spectre's head and donned it himself. It also provided a clue as to why he was now silent while a theme that could rouse him to great passion was being debated.

'Russia, I concede, is run by a permanent terrorist elite, but just consider Adolph, that celibate inhabitant of a modest Alpine chalet - a lover of dogs, music and architecture. He is no tyrant: more one of the oppressed!' Lewis glared at Vicky, willing him to raise another objection. Vickybird spluttered something, which went out like a defective candle. The Enemy delivered the coup de grace. 'The problem is entirely explained by the power of the Jewish financiers who are crushing us all down into the gutter.'

'You hate the Jews?' demanded Augustus, rallying belatedly to the stricken Neuburg.

'Hate?' repeated Lewis as if he did not recognise the word. 'Everything I do is done in cold blood, you know.' He smiled. 'I have the temperament of the duellist.'

This cocky declaration provoked a silence during which Augustus surveyed the company and found himself unhappy with what he saw. Beside him was Nina in her second-hand clothes with holes in the tights. Soon, he guessed, she would tell them she "must go home and dash off a drawing, what!" and simply translate herself to The Burglar's Rest. There was the gangling Neuburg with his high-pitched voice, frayed collar and stained tie, whose eyes, when they were not stealing adoring glances in the painter's direction, seemed to be seeking something that was not there. Opposite sat Lewis, sallow-skinned, puffy. The striking good looks that had distinguished him in the artist-hero days of Blast were gone. He was a victim of nephritis and failing sight, which were products of an ineptly treated pre-war dose of clap. This had already necessitated two operations and would soon demand a third.

With this in mind, the painter morosely examined the heap comprising Dylan and the Spectre. Her hand was dangling on his thigh while the poet's invisible own caressed more hidden contours. Augustus felt alarm. Later, he was certain, they would rut as carelessly as he had with Caitlin of the tawny mane and wild blue eyes that morning. Delia would lead Dylan back to her spacious flat on the Strand, where she worked as a call girl. Then, if the rumour were true that Dylan's days were French-lettered but the nights were not (he had never got the hang of it), infect him with the same bacillus ravaging Lewis, unless, of course, the Welshman were too legless to perform. Inspired by this happy thought, Augustus offered them all another drink, and everyone but the Enemy accepted.

'The pamphlets are written much as one talks, and nearly as fast,' he explained. 'To write they are often a chore. With my non-polemical writing it is the reverse and I have just such a work on the boil at present.'

Lewis and Augustus rose at the same time. Meanwhile Nina, inspired by gin and philandering nearby, jerked up her blouse to reveal a pair of breasts, unimpeded by a brassiere, that were surprisingly firm and well rounded. 'Modigliani said I had the best tits in Europe,' she declared, and so as not to disappoint the sea of faces staring at her, favoured them with a limerick:

'There was a young girl of Berlin
Who had a musical quim,

Hitler had her one night
And heard with a fright
"When the Saints Go Marching in."'

A half-amused, half-astonished murmur rippled round the crowded bar. Vicky blushed and planned his escape, but worse was to follow. Dylan, whose actor's instinct could never resist an audience, chose that moment to fling off hat and veil, and clamber onto the table. The crème de menthe trickling from the Spectre's toppled glass began to dye one shoe a sickly green, as he delivered the riposte he had been brewing for the just departed Lewis:

'Fascism is a cancer crabbed in the tomb of our time shredding the future with its claws. Even now, in the New Testament whites of your eyes, I see its tendrils shape a swastika and hear you fall in behind the glutinous drum of the dreadful German, which will hurtle you to no tangible destination, but speed for speed's sake, an iron train, streamlined and barbaric, bringing its freight of death on time.'

'I'm liking what you say, but not where you say it!' Kleinfeld had come round from behind the bar. The shoulders of this ex-Czarist officer were almost on line with the chest of the orator, who ignored him and continued:

'Fascism will clear the bats from your belfries and winch up your heart with razors. There'll be no forests only concrete; no coloured shirts just black ones...'

Kleinfeld's burly arms had ringed Dylan's waist and hoisted him from the table. Then, despite the protests of the music hall comedians, the landlord carried the poet across the bar, swung him through the door and deposited him on the pavement.

V°
La Tour Eiffel

There was no neon in Vicky's London. When he hurried outside, Charlotte Street was lit by streetlamps whose glow made even the shadows friendly. Spread-eagled on the pavement, Dylan was beaming up at the heavens like a child.

'Look how the moon is trailed by bands of urchin stars!' he sighed. 'Are those the Splendid Lights?'

It was not a London sky at all, more one that might be seen above the roofs of Rimini or Madrid. A group of people on the other side of the road was staring not up at the stars, however, but across at them. A very lanky man with frizzy hair that corkscrewed from his head, two elderly women and a young girl were standing outside Bertorelli's. The women wore long white vestments and the man a blue robe. A curious sound like that of a girder dragged over concrete echoed across the street. The clanking came from the man's six-inch iron foot, a physical feature that had led to him being dubbed Iron Foot Jack. He and his followers had just vacated the basement of a house in Charlotte Street; where naked they had been celebrating the rituals of his religion.

'Hail the Star-Imp who 'as fallen!' he boomed out.

'He bears the debris of Orion,' the oldest and shortest of the women added.

'Betelgeuse, actually,' said Dylan, hauling himself up onto his elbows. 'I took a celestial caravan to Orion once but didn't like it much. No beer.'

This startling news signalled the emergence of the Spectre, with veil akimbo and dress askew. Disappointed in their new messiah, the Children of the Sun shuffled sorrowfully off in the direction of the Square.

'I'm going to do a story - a nice one, you'll like it,' Dylan informed Vicky as he clambered to his feet. 'There'll be no worms or wombs, but a bug-eyed monster on Betelgeuse unanimously elected to referee the local form of rugby; they play with bits of each other up there, with their green feelers and antennae, and all.'

Cackling happily, Dylan swaggered up the street followed by the Spectre and Vicky. At the corner, they passed the restaurant de La Tour Eiffel, dimly lit and seemingly deserted, then turned into Rathbone Place. Ahead of them, the two varsity men seen earlier in the Fitzroy Tavern were cantering after a magnificent-looking woman dressed in a coat of tiger skin with matching cap, calico trousers, and black boots, whose five-inch stilettos remedied the shortness of her stature.

'There goes Betty Boop!' cried Dylan, as she, then the undergraduates, disappeared into the Wheatsheaf whooping like a hunting party. Vicky, who felt he had had enough of extravagant women to last a lifetime, hiccupped something about going home. 'Nonsense, man,' cried Dylan, hustling them all into the long narrow bar with the green upholstered tables and red linoleum covered floor. The woman was at the bar, giggling with the varsity men. Vicky recognised her. She had cast aside all suggestion of middle age, however. Cosmetics had not achieved this, for her face, with the finely etched jaw, flaring nostrils and panther-like eyes bore little make-up. It was due to an exotic quality, which the savage clothes underlined. She was the gardener who had delayed him that morning.

'You can almost taste the gin and lime of her breath from here,' said Dylan, 'and I've tasted it from there. She is Betty May, an artist's model who posed, though that is not the correct word, for 'Gus John and the rest of the racketeers. Before that, she was an apache dancer in Paris. She wrote a book an official bluestocking from the yellow press tried to ban.'

'Ah, so she's the tiger woman,' said Vicky. 'Don't be surprised I should have read it. I like to keep abreast.'

He laughed his extraordinary laugh, which some had compared to a hyena's. The screeches seemed to penetrate the wood-panelled walls, dotted with the tartans of the clans. 'I'm sorry,' he went on red-faced, 'I did not mean to be ostrobogulous.'

'She didn't write the book, she sponsored it,' said Dylan. 'It was really written by journo-literati Gilbert Armitage for forty quid. She has beseeched me to ghost an article for The News of the World. I will not be paid in money as such, but although she is no spring chicken that will not matter.'

The woman continued surveying them with her feline stare. Like courtiers, the undergraduates moved back so her view was unimpeded.

'You're much nearer than you think,' she announced unexpectedly, addressing Vicky in her husky voice.

Dylan's surprise was patent. 'You two know each other!'

'We're neighbours, actually,' stammered Vicky.

'I was Raoul Loveday's wife,' the woman said. 'That's why I know the look when I see it.'

'Wasn't he that actor chappie?' said the shorter of the undergraduates. His unruly quiff and goggling eyes gave him the appearance of a newly hatched chick.

'He was an Oxford man like you.'

'Who died in Sicily,' contributed Vicky.

'Yes,' agreed the woman, turning to him. 'The death certificate blamed enteritis brought on by local water, but I think it was drinking the blood of the cat they sacrificed what did him. He was weak anyway. He had lost pints of blood slashing himself with razors every time he said "I". Then there were all them drugs.'

'I say,' said the Chick.

'You wish you'd been there, don't you?' demanded Betty May.

Vickybird, the recipient of this question, was only half listening. He was wondering what the subject was of the conversation that was so earnestly engaging the Spectre and a skinny man with lank hair and bad teeth in the booth they had scurried to.

'At the Abbey; you wish you'd been there.'

1922 - The tedium of that sloppy life in Steyning with the Vine Press failing and a wife, who when she was not cuckolding him, was berating him for his inability to earn a living. Those long nights with the wind whistling through Chanctonbury Ring, a place only the stern, cold gods would visit, and all that while, Crowley had discovered at Cefalu the perfect backdrop for his craft. Vickybird forgot that the result had been a squalid ménage, in which the Beast supervised the Scarlet Woman's impregnation by a goat and was usually too shattered by heroin to get out of bed for the Adoration of the Sun. He saw only the Sicilian sun drilling the parched soil, conjuring up the hot gods Pan and Bacchus - the dreamscape of an adventure he had shied from like a frightened mare.

'At the funeral the Beast said Raoul had gone out like a match having lighted his cigar,' said Betty May. 'That's what types like you are, matches that he uses and tosses away. Yet you lap it up. Every moment carries the thought of him. He ruined your health. You see, I knew it. Squandered your money?'

Again, this was true: having exhausted his own inheritance, Crowley encouraged Vicky to part with almost all the money left him by his aunt. It went on publishing the slender volumes, with their vellum pages and gold bindings, of the Beast's poetry and magic, restaurant and hotel bills and the Richebourg wine and perique tobacco the Master favoured.

'Yet you're still lovesick, like a swain mooning over a milkmaid.'

'Shouldn't that be the other way round?' objected Dylan.

'I left him,' protested Vicky.

'Not in your heart. Though you know what he really is.'

'Great Raven digs up corpses and plays cricket with their shin-bones,' contributed Dylan.

'There was a diary, you know. I found it amongst Raoul's effects. I never told the press. The things in it were much too foul.'

'Oh, do tell, Betty!' Dylan implored.

However, Vicky could guess - the mixing of fluids; the peculiar dietary practice of eating what another had shed. How catholic were the tastes of magick!

'He called you a deformed and filthy abortion with no moral character. He said when God made you he broke the mould.'

A Victorian crank with mental gangrene, an Oscar tamed, chorused Dylan in his mind.

Vicky wished he had never met Crowley or turned with suspect glee the pages of Abra-Melin. He did not want to be there with this cat woman and Dylan amidst the fumes of beer and tobacco. He began to mutter his goodbyes, but Dylan forestalled him:

'A pint this time, Vicky?'

'Just a half,' he heard a voice squeak, his own hemmed in by a courtesy as destructive as it was outmoded. Prompting no response from Dylan, his politeness drove him to step out of the character he did not possess and shamble to the bar, where he tried to attract the attention of one of the two extremely quick and pretty barmaids. Beside him stood a skinny man with a large head, pale-blue eyes and a pencil moustache. He wore baggy grey flannel trousers and a leather-elbowed sports coat with a dark green shirt and hairy tie, and was staring at the undergraduates with loathing.

'Shrieking little poseurs,' he muttered in a rough-edged voice fighting its own plumminess. 'They're swamping the place just as they did the Fitzroy; nothing here but twits, parlour Bolsheviks and Welsh dog impersonators.'

'I'm a socialist myself,' said Vicky. 'What artist isn't?'

'Evelyn that's one, then there's old Ezra,' the man said, grasping the two pints of Younger's the barmaid had just set before him. He bore them off like Cup Final tickets to the far corner where a gruff, cloth-capped individual was waiting to play darts. It had been this same tormented old Etonian, who, in search of more authentic working-class surroundings, had led the exodus from the Fitzroy to the Wheatsheaf two years before. Now he was contemplating another such move but was confused as to which was better - the burglars at

The Black Horse, or the razor boys and Blackshirts at the Marquis of Granby.

Vicky ordered the round, conscious that the Spectre had attracted the interest of the varsity boys.

'Bit soon for the Chelsea Flower show, what?' the Chick gurgled, referring to the roses that had not yet fallen from her veil.

'Marigolds are tumbling from the clouds,' the Spectre, once more in oblique mode, replied.

'I say, that's awfully droll.'

The taller of the two had spoken. His hair, which was clipped shorter than the other's, gave him the air of a monk.

'Are you a poetess?'

'I am she that was and will be. I am Lilith, Jezebel and Typhoid Mary.'

'How jolly!' said the Chick.

'Only one Delilah at a time, boys,' cut in Betty May, baring her fangs. 'Anymore of this and I will have to fetch the whip.'

The students cooed. The Spectre drifted off in the direction of the toilet, fumbling in her handbag as she went. Vicky handed Dylan the pint and stood there uncomfortably cradling the crème de menthe with the undergraduates smirking - his own humble half-pint waiting forlornly on the bar.

'I did a degree once,' announced Dylan, thrusting out his jaw.

'You left school at seventeen!' objected Betty.

'I've got more degrees than a thermometer!'

'I'm reading Classics,' piped up the Chick.

'I'm reading Dashiell Hammett. However, I am forgetting my manners. Let me introduce myself. First and foremost, I'm Thomas, Dylan, a man in quest of a womb with a view - in fact, anything will do so long as it's nude and in a wet mackintosh. This is that well known prince of letters, Victor Neuburg, late of The Sunday Referee.'

'You mean the Victor Neuburg?' the Monk asked.

Vicky was flattered. Like Crowley, he had had his share of cultivating the young. Arthur Calder-Marshall, the novelist, had assisted him at Steyning; the New Zealand poet Rupert Croft-Cooke had had his work published by Vine Press. Both recorded their experiences. How had these students heard of him; through his work on the paper, or hope against hope, through The Triumph of Pan, out of print for over twenty years?

'You're the man Aleister Crowley turned into a camel,' announced the Monk.

Vicky wished a steamroller would crush him and his remains be fed to birds ignorant of his biography.

'That's right,' agreed Dylan. 'The Beast humped him in the desert.'

Birds would not do, I need crocodiles, thought Vicky. Nevertheless, he grinned his glutinous grin as the Spectre rejoined them, her face flushed by a disturbing brilliance.

'Whoever said cocaine is addictive was talking nonsense,' she twittered. 'I've been taking it for years.'

'Golly,' said the Chick.

'Where do you get it?' asked the Monk.

'It doesn't grow on trees, you know,' snapped the Spectre, her scarlet mouth spitting out the words faster than the lips could form them. 'It flourishes in mountains, high mountains, far away, over seas and rivers, brought by boats floating like crystal on the ultramarine waves. Try Brilliant Chang at the Forty-Three!'

'You boys are game for anything,' said Betty with a leer. 'But keep away from the white stuff. I was crazy for it until Bob came along and locked me in a room. Then I was crazier still, snarled, and scratched like a puma. It is a very big paving on the road to hell. Get me a drink, will you!'

Shoved out of the circle, the Chick obliged.

'An eddication,' reflected Dylan, sozzled and an imp, 'a straw boater, a hamper on the Isis, plus fours like sheets on washing lines - what wouldn't I give?'

'I don't know that I like your tone,' said the Monk.

'You mean the tone of my shoes or that of the russet that tinges my petal-strewn locks?' Dylan ruffled his hair coquettishly.

'Your manner of address is wanting.'

'I never wear tweed on Sundays, do you? Corduroy, brothel creepers and a tie with more hair on it than a gorilla are my manner of dress. You should really try to look seamier, you know. That's the thing these days - seaminess!'

The Monk lunged, but another hand interceded, one tanned and hooped by bracelets, which floated from his wrist to the back of his neck and massaged him out of Dylan's limelight.

'I think our poet needs a shot of fresh air,' Betty May hissed to Vicky, who taking the hint, drew Dylan towards the door. The poet collapsed instead into an alcove, taking Vickybird with him. Gazing blearily into the latter's face he gasped, 'I fear you Vicky and all Creative Lifers like the Boojum!' before slumping back. The Spectre joined them, her shoulder made a convenient pillow for the poet's head. Vicky thought he heard a machine-gun, but it was only Delia babbling on about her brother Steve, who was no good and was currently in the Scrubs.

Her words shattered against the bulletproof vest of their recipient's absorption in a dilemma. Why did he not lean slightly forward, raise himself, and with a polite farewell vacate the bar? At that moment Betty May, to general hilarity, was on all fours lapping up a saucer of Scotch, a turn originally made famous by Dylan, who, had he been awake would have been horrified at the plagiarism. However, Vicky's arms would not move and someone seemed to have nailed his leather soles to the floor. He took out his pen and doodled on the mat, Dylan's face, not a flattering portrait like John's, but one in which the jowls rehearsed their future beneath the dribble-glazed chin. While drawing, Vicky wondered if a shadow would fall across him and a taloned hand appear, proffering a napkin with the same face on it.

The barmaid's shout of last orders did nothing to rouse Dylan; but when her equally attractive colleague, who fitted the buxom description of her calling to a tee, removed his glass, the poet's hand shot out and seized the handle as though connected to it by invisible wires. 'Oh, loathsome curfew of the Capital Punishment,' he howled. He then urged the entire bar, now free of Betty and her students, to transfer their custom to the Marquis of Granby, which would be serving beer for half an hour longer. This was due to a quirk of the licensing laws, which allowed Holborn more time than Marylebone.

The scrum they joined had as its object a public house very different from both the Wheatsheaf and the Fitzroy Tavern. Against a backdrop of grimy walls draped with posters, spivs with thin moustaches, a knot of Blackshirts, and three guardsmen on the lookout for queers to beat up were waiting. They eyed with interest the slovenly types pouring in, of which Dylan, Vicky, and the Spectre, wafting like a figurehead through the Players' mist, were definitely the stars.

Careless of the razors that nestled in the pockets of the men he bumped into, the Welshman shoved his way forward to the horseshoe-shaped bar. He was met by the glare of the landlord to whom his pop-eyed face was not unfamiliar.

'None of your doggy tricks in here!'

'You are confounding me with my brother Evelyn, a travelling salesman, well known for his mental instability and habit of imitating poodles. I will have a pint and a half of Directors and...' Crème de menthe was not a well-known staple at the Marquis and a substitute did not come easily to mind, '...a half of cider, my good man.'

Once served, Dylan ferried the drinks back. A few feet away stood the Blackshirts, resplendent in the jackboots, breeches and Sam Brown belts of a uniform that had first been aired that day and would not be banned until November. So clad they had that afternoon marched to a park in Bow, where Mosley had harangued a crowd of many thousands with the news that fascist efforts would from henceforth be concentrated in the East End. Jews and lefties had stayed well out of sight, until now, that is, and the entrance of the hook-nosed man in the Norfolk jacket, his dishevelled companion, who bore all the hallmarks of a Left Wing Book club reader, and a female whose costume and state were an affront. The leader of the group, a squat individual with sly eyes began to shoulder his way over. His heftier colleagues followed him.

'Got a fag?' he had a steely voice that sliced like a razor.

Dylan, a physical coward, fumbled in his pocket, produced the Woodbines and pushed the flap open with his thumb. The Blackshirt reached forward and extracted the five remaining cigarettes, breaking a couple which fell crumbling to the floor.

'We should give this one a trim!'

'I have an appointment tomorrow first thing; the shortest back and sides in Bishopsgate. I've already auctioned the family comb.'

'That nancy-boy suit really is too small for you!'

'It is my brother Evelyn's, prone as many are aware to inexplicable lapses of taste. Yet he has sired fifteen children.'

Mystified, the Chief Black shirt turned on Vicky.

'Hail Mosley!' he barked.

'Lightning too,' said Vickybird.

'Are you taking the mick?'

'Sir Oswald is a man of splendid potential.'

Vicky, who had closely followed the fascist leader's career, with its dizzying U-turns, and hoped, as he hoped about Hitler, that it would all turn out to be an exercise in hubris, had spoken no more than the truth.

'He would have you lot on a banana boat to Madagascar,' the burly man immediately behind the chief growled.

'He has publicly declared such prejudice unBritish.'

'He's got to say that, hasn't he,' said the Chief. 'People aren't quite ready for the low-down on you Yids who've got the banks...'

'And the press!'

'And the courts!'

'I have very little,' objected Vicky.

'Still roasting those old chestnuts?' a mocking voice cut in. It was the petulant man with the face of a scarecrow Vicky had stood beside in the Wheatsheaf. He was obviously intent on martyrdom.

'Are you a Red?' demanded the leader.

'I see red when I hear the bilge you're talking.'

'You Bolshevik pansy,' hissed one of the Muscle, who lunged forward and grabbed the man by the lapels of his sports coat.

The Marquis was an ugly place with a reputation for violence. Not a month before a man had had his windpipe slashed by a razor. He had died in broad daylight on the same forecourt Vicky now found himself spilled out onto by the wave-like commotion rippling from the bar. In the confusion, he was separated from the others and the Blackshirts. The three off-duty guardsmen were standing nearby. One of them winked at him. The Blackshirts had surrounded his saviour and were warming up with insults before the big number, which would be a whirlwind of fists and razors. There was an expectancy in the air: the crowd was eager for a bloodbath. Vicky noticed two things: a pair of policemen approaching along Percy Street, whose pace quickened when they spotted the scuffle; and Dylan and the Spectre slinking across the street in the direction of La Tour Eiffel.

When, a short while later, Vicky entered the restaurant, he found himself in an L-shaped room with eight or nine tables, each with a white tablecloth and red lampshade, arranged around a three-tiered trolley. A huge brass urn filled with hydrangeas and ferns dominated the room: brass pots with drooping greenery hung from the ceiling. Vicky had never visited La Tour Eiffel in its Twenties heyday, when it had boasted the actress Tallulah Bankhead and the young Prince of Wales amongst its regulars, but even so the air of neglect was palpable. The lights were dimmed or in many cases their sockets bulbless. The foliage in the urns and pots was a dusty tangle. The tiers of the trolley, which had once sagged beneath mounds of caviar and Roquefort, now had little more to flaunt than an apple and a slab of mouldy cheddar.

Debt had driven Stulik, the kind-hearted and alarmingly corpulent proprietor to this pass, and he was at that moment pacing up and down with his hands behind his back, his moustaches adroop, his face yellowish-grey, muttering inaudibly to himself, while Chocolate, his dog, limped mournfully in the opposite direction. An old waiter, who also had seen better days, stood flicking his napkin and gazing glumly at the door. It had only opened twice that evening: first to admit Augustus John, then, more recently, Dylan and the Spectre, who had joined the painter at the table he occupied by the window. The entrance of the dishevelled newcomer did nothing to reassure Stulik that the restaurant's fortunes were on the mend.

'Is there going to be a scrap?' demanded Augustus who had parted the daffodil-yellow blinds and was peering out through the window.

'I think the constabulary have mustered,' said Vicky.

'Yes, the Goodge Street Runners are there, but the crowd's holding them back. What is this? One of the Blackshirts has that skinny bugger by the scruff of his neck and is going to slice him with a razor. No, he is saved. The coppers are hauling the thug off like a bit of meat out of the back of a lorry.'

'They stole my ciggies,' moaned Dylan.

Vicky fished the Gold Flake out of his pocket and pushed them towards the poet. Caught by the lamplight, one of the three stars on the packet flashed like a nova. Augustus was regarding him.

'Sorry about what Wyndham said. He is all blast you know. When he came back from America, it was the "Tycoon", before that the "Artist". Now fascism is his latest pose. I asked him once if such disguises were necessary. Was he a fugitive of some sort? Then I realised he was running from himself: an incurable romantic! Won't you join us? The duck should be good. I bought it myself only an hour ago.'

Such was Stulik's financial predicament that he sometimes had to ask customers to nip out for the eggs for their omelette. So Augustus had been sent to the backdoor of the Fitzroy Tavern, where he had haggled with the reluctant Kleinfield over a fresh Aylesbury duckling originally destined for the family's Sabbath dinner the next day. The painter pushed his entrée of stringy asparagus away, and poured a glass of claret for Vicky as the latter lowered himself onto the chair alongside.

'I drink to be more myself,' declared Augustus as the wine splashed from the bottle.

'I because I am thirsty,' smirked Dylan. 'Actually, drink enables me to connect with a part of myself that sober is missing. It adds dimension.'

'I've never thought about drink like that. Now hashish, which I've eaten in jam at those parties Moffat gives in his exotic flat in Fitzroy Square, that's dimensional. It enhances music, colours grow more vivid, the knot in a napkin or a word mispronounced, gives rise to bellyaches of laughter. Then in the silence, you can almost hear the clockwork of the universe ticking away. Alcohol, in comparison, merely removes our social skin.'

'It raises Pan,' said Vicky.

'You would say that, wouldn't you?' drawled Augustus, arching an eyebrow.

The waiter was hovering over them with the forlorn air of the last penguin in a colony.

'We'll all have duck,' said the painter, feeling no need to consult the others. 'Make mine well done, and be a bit more lavish with the almond and liver stuffing than you were last time.'

'Quatre canard a la John,' announced the waiter importantly, writing this down.

'Make mine bloody,' said the Spectre, who might have been referring to the state of her nose as snuffling she rose, and crossing the room, sailed through the alcove that led to the toilets.

Augustus took her exit as an opportunity to unburden himself: 'Dylan,' he began, 'I am not myself one renowned for caution when dealing with women, but in Delia's case a little prudence might be in order.'

'A Muse amongst mice,' declared the poet.

Augustus frowned. 'Did you notice Wyndham's eyes?'

'Blind as he's batty.'

'He contracted the clap in his twenties. It was treated, but badly, I am afraid. He is now in the tertiary stage. The bacillus is attacking his eyes and kidneys.'

Dylan tried to look sympathetic but seemed mystified by the relevance.

'Delia is a whore and not a particularly sanitary one at that. Some of her clients have the strangest peccadilloes. Forgive me for ramming such an unsavoury point home,' Augustus finished, smiling at the inadvertence.

She had returned lit with the frantic spirit of the powder that possessed her, which after launching a volley of gibberish that bemused the three men, deprived her of appetite when the food came. Vicky, however, consumed the duck with relish, along with a second glass of wine. This leant an optimistic hue to the dilapidated restaurant he shared with one great man and another marked, perhaps, for that same destiny. It was only when the bill came that this pleasant mood evaporated. Stulik hovered uneasily over them with an anxious expression that implied that the small plate he was holding bore a telegram announcing the death of a dear one.

'It is nod only for tonight, you understand?' the Austrian handed the plate to Augustus, who tossed it, with bill unopened, onto the table.

'Quite right, Rudolf. Now I'd like a dark treble rum with whisky and another round for my friends.'

Quickest off the mark was Dylan who ordered Guinness, the Spectre crème de menthe, and Vicky expressed himself happy with the third glass of wine the painter duly poured him. Stulik moved sheepishly away. Augustus reached down and nonchalantly unfolded the bill. The total was for a shocking forty-two guineas. Absent-mindedly, the painter began perusing the items as his hand foraged in the pockets of his jacket, waistcoat and trousers. He produced a bundle of papers, which included a couple of white five-pound notes of a size that vied with the napkins. There were some cheques. Amongst them one for two and a half thousand pounds signed by Emerald, Lady Cunard.

'What's this entry for mid-April?' Augustus demanded when Stulik had returned with the drinks. 'Three days of bed and three very expensive dinners? I was at Alderney!'

Stulik was crimson. 'De young lady said it would be an order.'

'The young lady?' repeated the painter.

'Miss Magnamara.'

The name roused Dylan from the stupor induced by mixing wine with beer. He stared at Augustus with an expression at once hostile and curiously defensive. The painter's puzzlement, meanwhile, seemed only to have increased.

'Was she alone?'

'She hat gentleman in her.' The sound groaned from Stulik as if extracted by the rack.

'I don't see why I should foot the bill for Caitlin's shenanigans. What was he like this gentleman?'

'Like Herr Thomas.'

'You mean he had curly hair and a music hall comedian's suit?' Then the penny dropped. He glared at Dylan. 'You stayed here with Caitlin!'

'In the first spring of love,' replied the poet. 'How is she? It is all of seven weeks since I have seen her! Is her hair grown grey?'

Augustus, who had stroked tresses of that tawny mane back from the sweat-beaded brow that very morning, began muttering to himself in Romany, a language peculiarly suited to expressions of homicidal jealousy.

'To think it was me who introduced you in the Wheatsheaf!' he finally declared.

'I would sleep with my daughter, if I weren't wed already to my niece,' parried Dylan in a not-so-oblique reference to the friendship that had sprung up between the painter and Caitlin's mother - a source of much gossip in its day. Singularly liberated from any scruples in matters of sex, the painter's last recorded exploit would be to crawl into bed with one of his daughters when well past eighty and find both her and his kâri unwilling.

Augustus rose, pulling the tablecloth with him so that he overturned his drink, an event that did nothing to lighten his mood.

'Keep your vile fingers off my seraph's quim!' he roared.

Love, frustration at being so far from the loved one, and the nagging suspicion that he could never afford her, roused Dylan to battle as nothing else. He also rose and moved to the aisle where he squared up against Augustus, both of them dancing like boxers, the one indeed Max Miller, the other a gypsy out of a Romany romance. Dylan lunged, and the painter, a keen pugilist, deflected the blow and landed a punch squarely on his adversary's chest sending him reeling sideways onto a chair, which overturned and toppled to the floor. Still astride it, Dylan's legs flapped uselessly up and down like the pincers of an upturned crab.

'Stulik!' barked Augustus. 'Ensure that item is removed from my bill or you will find my custom erased instead.'

Marching across the room, he snatched his panama from the hatstand and exited with a loud slam of the door.

Stulik came over and helped Vicky raise Dylan, muttering to himself as he did so.

'The Splendid Lights,' cried the Welshman, who seemed sorry to have lost his horizontal vantage. He was helped to his feet. Stulik, who was almost in tears, moved to the table and with one fat paw raised the bill to his face, while with the other he began to clump together the cheques and notes the painter had abandoned.

'Eleven pounds, fifteen shillings and seven penfiggs; that cost three nights in Miss Magnamara,' he stammered out at last, appealing to Dylan who was brushing the dust off with his hands.

'Did Paris balk at the fare to Troy? Did Abelard curse the price of postage? Have no fear, kind Stulik, the debt will be discharged.'

'You settle now?' Stulik's voice shook with the unusual timbre of hope.

Dylan turned to Vicky, his puppy eyes brimming with appeal, but his erstwhile editor was nearly broke.

'Not at this precise instant, but have no fear! My credit in the Capital Punishment is good, my word a Jubilee Bond. Forthwith I will see my brother Evelyn, who as anyone can tell you, has made his fortune in the City. He dotes on me as the sea upon the sky.'

He nudged Delia, who, a better actress than expected, took the cue, and having risen, let him tow her backwards towards the door.

'I expect he is at White's at this very moment,' beamed Dylan, 'puzzled as to what to do with wads of cash that he will press only too willingly into my grateful hands. Why such a sum is but a cup of tea to Evelyn!'

The door closed with a rattle. Stulik examined Vicky mournfully. 'He has brudder Evelyn?' Vicky shook his head. There was a groan. Stulik waddled painfully to the table furthest from the door, heaved his bulk onto the creaking chair, and cradled his head in his hands. Chocolate, who had padded along behind him, collapsed beside his master's feet and began to whine.

It was Vicky's turn to feel invisible. The waiter had vanished, and Stulik soon remedied his despair with a sleep so profound that rumbustious snores rumbled from the back of the room. Vicky's day, not French, but red-lettered certainly, was at an end. He had been in the swim but was now becalmed, with just the lees of the claret in his glass to remind him of the waves. Soon he would step outside and be one more nonentity among the hurrying mass, carried back to Boundary Road and the silent reproaches of Runia, as, like a boa constrictor a cow, she digested the news that he had managed to squander the funds destined for the Comment Treasury. Knowing it would be a very long time before he would be permitted a drink again, he drained the last of his glass. He took a final look round the dingy but splendid establishment that Nancy Cunard, the dissolute daughter of Emerald, had christened "our carnal-spiritual home". As he did so he realised he was no longer alone. A shape was lurking among the shadows beyond the doorway leading to the stairs. Stepping into the light, a portly, shaven-headed man clad in a green kilt, ruffled blouse, and a jacket cut to the waist was revealed. It was the being who had infected that same Nancy Cunard with blood poisoning after biting her wrist with the tooth he kept specially sharpened for such serpent kisses. It was Victor Neuburg's nemesis.

'Do what thou wilt shall be the whole of the Law,' bleated Aleister Crowley in a distinctly nasal whine.

VI°
Great Raven

If by his costume Crowley had intended to evoke their first meeting, he was badly mistaken. The kilt was threadbare and the jacket bore a large hole in the left-hand sleeve, produced by a burning chimble of hashish. However, it was not just the clothes that accentuated the change: it was equally the bloated physique, the sallowness of the skin and rheuminess of the eyes. In fact, the presence of his old follower, in the hotel in which he had enjoyed Stulik's credit for the last month, came as a complete surprise to Crowley; in as much as anything could perturb a man who believed he had established a unique relationship with the universe. As far as he was concerned, a telephone number or even a misprint on a menu tallied in a mysterious fashion with his being.

'Do what thou wilt shall be the whole of the Law,' he bleated, a little louder this time.

The words received no answer from Vicky, but Stulik woke with a start: 'Brudders and sisters go to Ped. I vant to sleep,' he mumbled before his head slumped back onto his arms. Crowley had his litany, and at this time of night, the Viennese had his. The Beast, meanwhile, was awaiting his answer and this, most definitely, was not it.

Vicky knew he had only to intone seven simple words to satisfy the man who had been his master. He also knew that were he to say them "had been" would be "was", but his tongue, responsive to a long-suppressed desire, struck an 'l' against the palate.

'Love is the law, love under will.'

Just a small courtesy, thought Vicky, clutching at this straw as he had at so many others. However, he did not like the smile that lit Crowley's features, though it was not one of triumph - more like that of a man who had been in the desert too long and is offered water.

'De sooner you go de bedder I ligk you. Ged oud blease.'

Stulik had roused himself to more effect this time: he actually seemed to recognise the people he was glaring at. Nevertheless, the effort proved too much for him and his head once more sagged.

Moving his left arm up in a hieratic gesture then bringing one finger to his lips, Crowley padded over to the bar, from whose shelves he removed a bottle. Then, with an equally prosaic signal, he beckoned to Vicky to follow. The latter did so, followed by a low growl from Chocolate, which pursued them out through the alcove and up the first flight of stairs.

On the landing, they passed two private dining rooms: the first dust-lined, full of mahogany furniture and dying aspidistras; the second decorated by three faded panels, which, with their bold diagonals and spindly figures frozen in athletic postures, recorded the forgotten anger of the Vorticists.

'Wyndham's daubs,' sneered Crowley.

It occurred to Vicky to mention he had passed part of the evening with the author of the panels, but Crowley knew how star struck he was and would easily cap this with a greater feat of name-dropping.

On the second floor, they paused before two doors in need of paint, on the side of the building that faced the street. Crowley's womanish hand turned the handle of the right-hand one, and they entered a sombre habitation with a double bed, a shag-pile rug and heavy Bierdemayer furniture. The air was impregnated with the sticky scent of incense, the room strewn with articles that testified to the many callings imposed upon a man who would be magus.

A battery of test tubes, a Bunsen burner and retorts cluttered the surface of a chest - not alchemical apparatuses, but instruments necessary in the manufacture of his Elixir of Life pills. Crowley came, after all, from a long line of fanatically devout Plymouth brewers, which explained not only his apocalyptic obsessions, but also the fact that heredity had at last caught up with him, leading him to devise an altogether stranger brew than that of his forefathers.

Piled alongside both sides of the chest were books: not ordinary books but volumes which Vicky's cultivated eye saw were buckram-bound and vellum-paged with gold binding on the spines that glinted dully in the dowdy light of the bedside lamp. These expensive tomes were editions of almost all the fifty or so works the Beast had privately printed up until then.

They included his Hail Mary, which consisted of fifty hymns to the virgin and had been commended by the Catholic press under the misapprehension that it had been written by a famous actress; and his paean to sodomy, The Scented Garden. Then there were magical treatises, published at great expense, which invoked the Guardian

Angel or outlined, in suitably occluded language, the exact role of a Scarlet Woman. Finally, there were collections of short stories, many featuring the psychic detective Simon Iff, and novels, which apart from The Diary of a Drug Fiend, the public had resolutely ignored.

Near the chest, a low, rectangular table, surrounded by cushions, bore other visiting cards of a man whose occupations were myriad to the point of madness. There was a voodoo doll, wrought in ebony, with a scarred and singularly unpleasant face that glared up at Vicky. Hanging from the doll's arms were three smaller heads, the eyes closed, the features perfect, which Vicky also took as dolls, though something told him they were not.

The doll, these faces, and the garish African spread that covered the bed suggested an explorer was the tenant of the room; an assumption unsupported, however, by the contents of the wardrobe, one door of which had swung slightly ajar. Chinese silk robes, velvet cloaks emblazoned with masonic badges, a black flapper's dress with tassels, and a double-breasted suit hung within. These costumes, complemented by the fez and solar topee on top of the wardrobe, would have done credit to a theatrical costumier. They spoke eloquently of the protean nature of their owner. An easel and some canvases stacked alongside the window opened up vistas of yet another line.

Crowley shut the door behind them and turned to Vicky. 'I always knew you would come,' he beamed; 'and tonight of all nights!'

At a loss, Vicky began examining a black brassiere dangling over a chair. This, along with the skirt in the wardrobe and a collection of lipsticks, perfumes and mascara that covered one of the bedside tables, made him wonder just how far Crowley's celebrated transvestitism had gone. 'What a delightful artefact is the brassiere,' he said. 'It has contributed to far more joy than the gas-filled airships of Count Zeppelin. It is incapable of dropping any but the sweetest bombs. The inventor's name shall be mentioned in the Honour's List of the All High.'

'Still all folderol and T.A.P., is it Vicky?' said Crowley, arching one of his satanically barbered eyebrows.

'Take a pew? Why, yes.'

'Then why don't you!' roared the Beast. 'Can you still do Prayana?'

It was said genially, not like a command at all. Vicky sank down on the cushions, and crossing his legs, attempted to assume the required posture.

'A little stiff, eh!' laughed Crowley, going over to the bedside cabinet. Opening it, he removed two balloon glasses, which he filled from the bottle he had filched. He came over and proffered one to Vicky.

'I've already quaffed rather a lot tonight.'

Crowley drew back as though insulted: 'I will not try to deceive you into believing that this fine Armagnac is lacking in the oomph I tried to convince you once that pastis lacked. It is, however, an excellent libation for celebrating reunions. Drink it! Let us toast an occasion as unexpected as it is auspicious.'

Vicky did not like this at all, but took the glass and clinked it against Crowley's. The latter arranged himself upon the cushions opposite, assuming an identical posture. He is trying to hypnotise me, thought Vicky, as the horn-coloured eyes drilled into him. However, they were watery and weak, exerting as much force as the puffs of a train that is running out of coal.

'A lot of water under the bridge,' Crowley said at last, a comment that struck Vicky as weary. 'Here, look what I've been doing.' With the enthusiasm, though not the agility of a schoolboy, he heaved himself to his feet and shuffled over to the window, where he leafed through the stack of paintings, selected one and brought it over. Waved under Vicky's nose were swirling brushstrokes of scarlet and green depicting what appeared to be a pair of buttocks, one of which had been flogged and the other injected with a substance that had made it swell out of all proportion. 'This is what Blake was striving for,' said Crowley. 'Come! Look! There are more! Trance states all of them. Have seen anything like them?'

Vicky stiffly rose, followed the artist and was forced to agree that he had not. The first canvas was of three red-cowled monks leading a black goat up a mountain pass. Next, there was the torso of a female whose breasts and belly were exaggerated in a way that could have provided an Institute of Pathology with years of investigation.

'Ether,' Crowley pronounced the word with reverence. 'I and the model, we'd both inhaled.' He flipped the canvas forward to reveal another on which a man's hastily daubed face was struggling for features. 'Aldous commissioned it in Berlin but never came to collect. I had a big show. Porza Galleries. Seventy-three paintings and drawings were hung.' He forgot to add that none were sold. 'Yes, I've had my troughs. The yellow press has done its best to make me its whipping boy. I have endured the calumnies of tarts like Betty May. However, overall the years have not been so bad. Take the books, for instance. I expect there are a lot you haven't seen.'

Vicky, nevertheless, had not only seen but read the first work that Crowley liberated from the pile beside the chest. It was a copy of Magick in Theory and Practice, printed in Paris, the only edition to date. Vicky had reviewed it for The Referee and said as much. 'Favourably, too,' Crowley beamed at him, and then placing the book back on the pile, selected another work. This was the first volume of the Confessions. On the white cover, it bore a self-portrait of the author at his most demonic and his oversized signature, the A for Aleister shaped like a phallus with balls. 'Special edition,' said Crowley. 'There were only fifty bound like this. Numbered and signed!' He opened the flap to reveal a smaller version of the signature, the number 33, and the words The Spirit of Solitude. 'Two guineas is so little to ask!'

Possessed of the cunning of a bookseller, the Beast seized an attaché case that lay upright alongside the bed. 'In here is the pinnacle of everything I have striven for!' he said, opening it and taking out a book cradled in a velvet cloth, which he quickly unwrapped. The book bore on its embossed cover the title The Equinox of the Gods. 'It contains a full text of The Book of the Law as well as a brief history of my ascent to the thrones of the Secret Chiefs. And look!' he turned the leaves to a page that reproduced in colour an Egyptian stele. 'It is the Stele of Revealing, numbered 666 in the Cairo Museum, where Rose led me to it.'

Vicky, an experienced proofreader, noticed that someone had substituted an "l" for the "a".

'Damn it, you're right!' muttered Crowley. 'Well, "Revelling" reads just as well as "Revealing" to my mind - almost the same thing, at least as far as women are concerned. It seems to me you are missing the point. What was the result of the first publication of this work in 1912?'

As far as Vicky could remember, the book had made no impact on the British public whatsoever.

Crowley put him right. 'The outbreak of the Balkan War, which occurred exactly nine months later. And what did the appearance of the second edition in 1913 inspire?'

'The Great War?' suggested Vicky dubiously.

'Exactly, The third came out nine months before the Sino-Japanese, currently breaking up the Far East! What then can this fourth edition presage but the triumph of Horus, the "Warrior Lord of the Forties"? Just think! The gospel of the new Aeon for thirty bob.'

The door opened to admit a woman. She was wearing a dress of scarlet satin, which curved lasciviously around her ebullient bosom and equally magnificent hips. This gave way to black openwork stockings and tapering four-inch heels that emphasised the shapeliness of her calves. Tresses of glossy black hair framed her dark luminous eyes and carmine painted lips. With her into the room entered an aura of something wild and sultry, redolent of the vice-ridden waterfronts of Havana or Tangiers.

Heedless of Vicky, she sauntered, all swaying rump and slung back shoulders, across to Crowley, and instantly they began to smother each other with kisses of such intensity that it seemed soon they would get down to the real business of eating each other.

'My Gitana, my Saliya,' cried Crowley, snatching a breather, in a voice whose reediness belied the virility of the sentiments. 'I shall have you in the summer and the south, with our passion in your body and our love upon your mouth.' The Beast's hands gripped the woman's buttocks, his talon-like nails threatening to rip the fabric. 'Did you prosper?' he hissed.

'No-one wants the leedle pills,' her mouth blew out the husky words like smoke from a cigarette. 'I try Harlequin and Forty-Three. The liquor of life I say them. Maybe three guineas is too many.'

'You cyst squeezed out of the rotting fleshpots of Rio,' Crowley roared. He raised his arm, and bringing the fist full down on her face, sent her sprawling onto the floor. 'Who needs cheese, monthlies and pox, you chewer of cocks?'

The Beast had demonstrated the capacity of his verse to switch from romance to scatology in a trice, for these words echoed the spirit of the yet unpublished Leah Sublime, which he had composed in three hours on a June morning in 1920. "I think I'll collect all my filth in one poem,' he had written at seven. "I think I did," he had concluded at ten.

Crowley crouched down beside the woman on the shag-pile rug. He gripped her by the waist, flipped her over and pulled her up until she was kneeling. Then, nonchalantly, like a man drawing a blind, he tugged the dress up, revealing a pair of pistachio knickers - ice-cream colours were all the rage - and suspenders that ran from the stocking tops towards the belt that girdled her midriff. He reached forward and yanked the knickers to one side, granting Vicky a dizzying vision of a bush of black hair. With his other hand, the Beast lifted the front of his kilt. The lack of any further fumbling confirmed the authenticity of his disguise. Crowley plunged forward with a whoop, concealing the crouching woman's rear behind pumping folds of green tartan. Vicky left the cushions and slunk towards the door.

'Be with you in a jiffy,' cried Crowley, who had schooled himself to remain objective even in the most delirious of situations.

The woman's moans had changed to pants as Crowley abruptly drew back, and pressing down on her hips, plunged forward again. The woman screamed. The Beast, Vicky realised, had breached the unmentionable vessel - his lusts as ever fundamental. In the same way, he had compelled Vicky to possess him in the desert, his body arched in pathic bliss. However, Vicky had not been himself but Pan, his noiseless hoofs trembling on the sand as he had exploded into an emptiness where nothing would come of it - the very point of the exercise - and Crowley had adored him.

The Beast seemed stricken, his eyes glazed over: 'The seer is in the seer,' he intoned hoarsely. The last word rattled into a gasp as he celebrated another useless orgasm.

He had said the same words with Vicky. They were taken from the Holy Hymn to Hermes and are spoken at the climax of the sexual ritual to invoke the God. However, no inviolate form appeared in that second-floor hotel room; no mysterious breeze blew through the partially opened window and cooled the brow of Thoth. With a dissatisfied grunt, the Beast clambered to his feet and stated in a detached, empirical tone, 'Meagre, localised and half-hearted. No point in collecting the fluids.' He landed a kick on the woman's behind.

There was a knock at the door. Certain it was the management, Vicky stiffened. Mumbling to himself in Arabic, Crowley shuffled over and opened it. For a few moments, he exchanged unintelligible greetings with the visitor, and then flung the door open. A man in his late thirties, with a sharp charcoal grey suit, slicked-back fair hair and a protruding nose strode into the room. He did not remove his brown trilby, and disdaining the cushions, sank into an armchair. The presence of Vicky and the supine woman with the hitched up skirt seemed a matter of complete indifference to him.

'I have these fabulous Brazilian cheroots blessed with the highest nicotine content in the world,' Crowley said effusively. He took up the humidor, that along with a chess set occupied the surface of the table at the foot of the bed, but the visitor declined both cigar and the drink that was then offered, despite Crowley's urging: 'An exquisite Armagnac; picked it up at my merchant today; bugger the expense!'

'The rendezvous with Neptunus is proceeding smoothly,' the newcomer said in a voice as clipped as the words it tidily arranged.

The news produced a curious effect on Crowley. His face took on an absent air. When he spoke, it was as though he were repeating something he himself was hearing: 'The Oracle of Dawn is Brilliance,' his voice trilled the last syllable.

'And the time?' the man demanded.

'The Hour of Dawn is Six Two Two. The Omen is Riches.'

The man nodded. This all seemed perfectly clear. 'And the location?'

'The Place of Dawn is the obelisk of Thothmes.'

A short exchange followed in Arabic - the only word intelligible to Vicky being "Simpson". He supposed this to be a reference to the store in Piccadilly. Appearing satisfied, the man rose.

'How's Bessie?' Crowley asked.

'She's had a touch of distemper. Her fur is falling out. But she's cheerful.' The man said before exiting as smartly as he had come in.

'Now, Saliya, let me help you up,' said Crowley, turning to the woman.

'Demon!' came a hoarse moan from the carpet.

'I but serve my great Master Lucifer,' said Crowley, whose tongue was always firmly in his cheek - and anyone else's for that matter - on the question of Satanism. 'Ask this man, Whore of the Stars!' he indicated Vicky. 'He was present at that august council composed of Beelzebub, Asmodeus, and Baal.'

The grisly visages of the princes of hell that had paraded before them in 124 Victoria Street had been visible only to Vicky - Crowley could just make out vague shapes.

His solicitude exhausted, the Beast foolishly turned his back on the woman. With a speed that astonished Vicky, she sprang to her feet and pounced, digging her scarlet nails into the back of the shaven head. Blood trickled from the welts. Howling, one hand to the wound, Crowley spun round and slapped her so hard she was hurled onto the bed. 'Blood, me, would you, prick-struck cunt of reeking pus!' he roared, a sentiment accompanied by his seizing of her shoulders, the loss of one shoe as she was dragged across the carpet, and her despatch through the door with a well-aimed kick.

Crowley turned the key in the latch and went over to the humidor, removing a cheroot, which he began rolling between his fingers. Vicky alerted him to the blood oozing down the back of his head. Crowley tutted, and going to the Armagnac spilled some onto his hands and patted it in as a man does aftershave, only a flicker at the corner of his mouth betraying the pain. 'Brandy's better,' he said.

A muffled but definitely hostile sound came from the other side of the door.

'Clap-rotten hell bitch,' muttered Crowley, who going to the shoe, picked it up, marched to the door, turned the key, opened it, and hurled the projectile out provoking a shrill scream. Then, locking the door once more, he sucked on the cheroot, the pungent fumes briefly banishing the all-pervasive Ruthvah, and smiled as though satisfied by recent events. 'Let me refresh your drink,' he said to Vicky.

'A bottle of Bass a day is my usual ration,' answered the reluctant voyeur, 'and today I've had a tankful.'

'You never had much of a head for anything, did you? Heights made you dizzy, sea voyages sick, and two glasses of wine prompted you to make disgusting propositions to the first woman you met. Your disposition was uniquely favoured for the Work - never, except for perhaps on one occasion, did I encounter anyone with your mediumistic powers. However, you lacked stamina and will. You not so much handed on the torch as hurled it from your squeamish fingers at the first hint of a spark, Lampada Tradem!'

'My hands were burnt,' protested Vicky.

'By your own fear! Bah, you don't need Armagnac, you need Kublai Khan Number Two.'

So saying Crowley walked over to the chest and selected from the many medicine bottles that lined it, one glazed a smoky blue. Filling two glasses with the black viscous liquid it contained, he turned and offered one to his guest. Vicky refused because whatever the drink contained – and in fact, it was a cocktail composed of gin, vermouth and opium - the suspicion that drugs had produced all the visions haunted him. Gods and spirits with unspeakable names had appeared before him; but how could he know if they were anything more than apparitions induced in a mind so parched of illumination, it would do anything to achieve it?

'As long as drugs are used those whirling bands of light, those entities, with the heads of falcons or lizards, can be refuted,' Vicky stammered out.

'Ye Gods!' snorted Crowley with disgust. 'You might as well say to an astronomer that because he uses a telescope his conclusions will be false.'

'Then it was all real!' said Vicky. 'I have asked myself for years.'

'Faith,' roared the Beast, now thoroughly exasperated, 'that is always what you lacked. It was all there and is there still.' His arms reached out and embraced the room in a hieratic gesture. 'The air is thicker with Spirits than the summer with flies.'

'Actual Spirits?' demanded Vicky; 'beings with a substance independent of our own?'

'I gave you Bishop Berkeley,' groaned Crowley, 'I gave you The Hunting of the Snark. You learnt from them, as you did from the Vedas, that reality is arbitrary. Do you not realise yet? The mind is the enemy and if by summoning a vision of something that cannot exist you rebuke it, well and good - you are halfway to breaking the chains.'

'Then it makes no odds if what we see is really there or not?'

Vicky wondered why he felt such alarm at the doubt that had usurped conviction in the Beast's watery eyes as he answered: 'During our association I was sure that what we were evoking operated independently of ourselves. Then, in America, a land haunted only by the Red Indian, for it is difficult to believe its present occupants could leave much in the way of a spiritual trace, I wavered. I began to think that Aiwass, Ab-ul-Diz, and every familiar I had raised, including the great Gods and the Guardian Angels of the Watchtowers, Ol Sonuf Vaoresagi, were figments mustered by the drugs I had used to gain their knowledge and conversation. Now, however, I am once more firmly of the conviction that they have an existence as sovereign as your own.'

A flawed comparison: Vicky's being had long been eclipsed by the speaker's.

'Then you still don't know.'

'O Bes,' groaned the Beast. 'O Moloch and Zoroaster I pray you, render incapable forever of the joys of Ishtar this importunate one, were he no other than the fierce and warlike Bartzabel himself!'

Vicky screamed.

'You see!' cried Crowley, hopping in triumph from one foot to another; 'magick works!'

'Only too well,' replied Vicky for the second time that day. 'It was Bartzabel who killed Ione. Why did you not release me from him?'

'It was right she should die. She was a lunar vampire to whom you succumbed. She would have brought you worse horrors than any I inflicted on you. Besides, it was neither you nor Bartzabel who killed her. I went to the door of that studio in Flood Street and drew an astral T to symbolize her treachery. She was blasted by my curse.'

'You wanted her yourself. Someone saw her massaging your scalp.'

'I have spilt the milk of the stars in so many, it is hardly surprising I cannot remember if she were a vessel or not,' said the Beast wearily.

'Oh, but you would remember, just as Bartzabel remembers me,'

Crowley scrutinised him with professional interest as Vicky described the streets heaped with rubble, the distant flashes and drones of aeroplanes, the screams and the explosions.

'And what are these visions?' Crowley demanded: 'figments created by your mind, which is obviously still somewhat unbalanced, or a window on the future?'

'I don't know,' said Vicky.

'Oh, but you do!' insisted the Beast, his voice rising to the rousing warble he reserved for The Book of the Law. "I am the warrior Lord of the Forties. The Eighties cower before me and are abased."' He paused, relishing Vicky's consternation, before saying, 'would you like to be released?'

'More than anything,' admitted Vickybird.

'By six twenty-two tomorrow morning I can have you free of it.'

'I should be missed at home.'

'Then go on with it! Unbanished, a Spirit as powerful as Mars festers like a cancer eating away at its host. Currently you glimpse the future, but soon your visions will be beyond reason. You will witness utter horror.' Sensing victory, Crowley smiled. 'Now will you have a Kublai Khan?'

Vicky once more refused.

'God, Victor, how dreary you've become. Apart from Datura and the Calabar Bean, we must have taken every substance in the book.' Crowley drained the glass and refilled it with more of the black liquid. 'Do you really no longer believe in the chemical gateway to the stars?'

It was a tired question. The Beast still saw the colours and dreamt the fantastic dreams, but his mind had become impervious to the nuances of the substances he used - he might as well have taken aspirin. 'Bah, the fundamental problem about drugs is that they tend to obsess you. Take heroin and cocaine. I have not much to thank them for, yet it is for them I crave. Whereas ether, hashish, opium and mescal, which I associate entirely with pleasure, I can take or leave. I begin to have a grave suspicion that there is a "will to suffer" at the root of it all. If I have erred, it is in going too far; the worship has become forced. I must be as capable of employing these means of grace as an engineer of mixing explosive chemicals.'

In his description of the irrational Crowley was fond of scientific metaphors. It was not this that struck Vicky, however; rather it was the doubt pleading to be contradicted. At sixty, broad-shouldered and obese, the Beast still possessed an aura as sinister as his reputation. However, something was dwindling, as though his girth was but a shell that would crack and fall away revealing a shrunken man with perplexed eyes.

'Have I ever done anything of value?' Crowley suddenly went on. 'Or am I a mere dabbler, existing by a series of sleights-of-hand?'

Vicky, who had more reason than most to cry Guilty, was puzzled as to why the pity he now felt disturbed him more than all the other feelings he had registered on the bands of an emotional spectrum that had ranged from adoration to loathing.

'You have written the greatest work on magic since the Renaissance,' he heard himself saying.

'Do you really think so?' purred the Beast. 'Nevertheless, even when smiling at the doubts of people who expect me to bewitch their pets, I doubt if I am such a great magician after all. The fact is, I possess the power of causing spiritual crises. That is, of course, all that ever happened. Produce your crisis in the man and the rest follows. You, Lampada Tradem, are very much a case in point. Bah! Madame Fatima Crowley! That is all I am fit for - to wiggle my leg in the air!' and this is precisely what he did, the tartan-socked limb performing a passable imitation of a belly dancer's toe turning.

Vicky found himself transfixed by the area below the hem of the kilt. The knees were blistered and red with carpet burns incurred by the Beast in his exertions with Saliya. Crowley followed his gaze. 'Can't have that!' he tutted, and moving over to the wardrobe, he swung open the door, and peered at the costumes hanging on display.

Reaching up, he unbuttoned his shirt, and running his fingers behind his neck, removed a chain with a rose and cross studded with five rubies. With it on, he had arranged with himself to act in one character; with it off in another. He continued in his perusal of the costumes, wondering whether to be Prince Choia Khan or Brother Perdurabo. In the end, he settled on a jacket emblazoned with a garter-like star and a stiff pair of black trousers with a silk stripe running down the seam.

Taking no notice of Vicky, he stripped off his clothes, revealing a feminine figure with nascent breasts, and donned the new costume, putting the chain back on as well. He had relegated Lord Boleskine to the closet. Now Crowley boasted the costume that went with a title, which, incredibly, he was entitled to bear - the Ordo Templi Orientis, an order of German occultists whose sex magick he had anticipated, had given it to him. The majority of them had regretted their involvement with the Holy King of Ireland, Iona and all the Britons ever since. Relishing the absurdity Crowley said: 'Ah, my phoenix lives: I have bagged women, butterflied in society, hunted tigers, hob-nobbed with dukes and cut-throats.'

'You were a chess Blue and your mountaineering feats are legendary,' purred Vicky.

Amazed by his own versatility, the Beast drew himself up and roared, 'I am aflame with the brandy of the thought that I, Saint E.A. Crowley, am the sublimest Mystic in all history, the Word of the Aeon, the self-crowned God whom men shall worship and blaspheme until the twilight of Crowleyanity, two thousand years hence!'

VII°
Gargoyles

Two people were sitting in the shadows of Buhler's. One was the man in the brown trilby last seen in Crowley's hotel room. After serving under him, Ian Fleming would paint him as the ruthless 'M' of the Bond books. Now an altogether different side of his nature was revealed as he gazed coquettishly across the table at the possessor of wavy black hair and saturnine features, which allied with a certain hauteur, gave their bearer the look of a defrocked priest. This was Tom Driberg, currently writing the William Hickey column at the Daily Express.

His drawl was like a bishop's as he said, 'Hammer will be chugging into Victoria about now. He'll bell my office when he reaches the hotel.'

His listener nodded. 'Would you have lunch with me tomorrow, Tom?' There was a note of pleading in his voice.

'Sorry, old man, I'm at the Dorchester with an oilman.' Driberg sighed. 'The Beaver wants no more stories of the "enchanting Lady

Chalice has mislaid her mink" variety. From now on, the column must devote itself to the doings of ordinary people. Unfortunately, the Beaver seems to believe those to be a group of Canadian swells whose lives are as dull as Vancouver.'

'We could make it cocktails?'

Driberg sipped the froth from his coffee and took an equally dainty pull on a black Balkan Sobranie. 'I'm to meet A.C. in Gerrard Street?'

'Yes. His carpet weaving is so intricate we could have another botch on our hands like the Pollitt business.'

'Then why are we using him?'

Apart from Madame Buhler, safely out of earshot at the cash register, the café was empty. Nevertheless, the man leaned forward. 'The Abwehr know it's become too dangerous to go on using diplomatic channels with the American. It was easy to sell them the idea that A.C. could be the conduit. Who would believe a character as outrageous as him could be an agent? There might be a lot of work for him in future if he tones down the maverick stuff.'

'He hasn't been to Russia for years; and that was with a troop of goodtime girls!'

'I don't mean the Soviets. He renewed his links with Canaris when he was living in Berlin. The Admiral thinks A.C. could be useful. Some of the key figures in the Nazi hierarchy are occultists. Why, you wouldn't believe ...,' a shutter had pulled down. The genial man of a moment before was gone.

'What wouldn't I believe, Max?' Driberg was stern - a priest extracting confession.

'If I tell you, you must swear on your heart of hearts not to reveal it to a soul. We're feeding Hess, the deputy Fuehrer, A.C.'s horoscopes

'...' the man's voice trailed off then started up again as though there had been a power failure. 'Have you tried that new place everyone's talking about beside the river...?'

Driberg yawned. 'So you're really going to put the boot into the Yank?'

'If it's the only way to show him what she really is.'

'Maybe he knows already. Maybe he's the same.'

'Either it's all hushed up and she goes back to Baltimore or we prosecute. She won't be much use to him in jail.'

'Have you seen them together? He's like her lapdog.'

'I'll be doing just that very shortly when filling in as equerry. Fruity Metcalfe had a surfeit of champagne and oysters at a January Club dinner last night.'

'Bunch of fascists!' Driberg growled and gazed out of the window. A top-hatted man had emerged onto the street. 'There he goes: the last of the Edwardians.'

Crowley was waving down a cab with his cane. With him was the gangling man who had been in the room. What did he have to do with anything? Captain King disliked chains, in which he did not know all the links. He asked Driberg who the man was.

The journalist shrugged. 'Hardly looks like the Beast's latest flame.'

'Do you still love him, Tom?'

'Love? It was never love,' insisted Driberg. 'It's true A.C. exerts a certain fascination. Got you hot under the collar for a while, didn't he, Max? You'd be better asking if he loves me!'

The driver of the cab was dubious as he received the key to the city from the Sage of the Labyrinth himself.

'The Gargoyle, Merde Street,' barked Crowley.

'Ain't that Meard Street?' the cabbie objected.

'To each his own,' was the smug response as the Beast sank back onto the plush, leather-lined seat and placed his case and steel-tipped Malacca cane next to him. 'The Gargoyle's one of the few places in London not hidebound by petty Anglo-Saxon restrictions. I think you will like it, Victor, if there is anything left of the man I used to know!'

At the top of Tottenham Court Road lights still blazed from the multi-coloured theatres, but the jugglers and conjurors who performed for pennies had deserted the pavements, as had the vendors of ices and jellied eels. There was a smell of chips, horse dung and toffee as they crossed Giles Circus and hurtled down Charing Cross Road.

'It's extraordinary you should turn up,' Crowley said, 'a real example of sympathetic magick. What, by the way, did you make of my friend?'

Vicky was at a loss. 'Perhaps you were a little harsh,' he stammered out eventually.

'Not that pox-ridden Brazilian strumpet!'

'Steady on, Guv'nor,' the cabbie said from the front.

Crowley leaned irritably forward and slammed shut the glass partition. He spoke next in almost a whisper. 'I meant Captain King. Not his real name, of course.'

'He seemed a most distinguished gentleman.'

'Never much of a judge of character, were you, Victor? The Captain came to study under me with a toad of a writer called Dennis Barleybollocks, who just wanted background for the execrable bilge he writes about black magic. With Max...ahem, Captain King, it went deeper. Like you, he had flair for the uncanny; like you, he reneged. He transferred his affections to nature. The way he can tell whether a squirrel or a woodpecker stripped a pinecone is quite uncanny. He lives in Dolphin Square in a flat that doubles as an office, with bush babies, a baboon, a grey parrot who uses the filthiest language you've ever heard, not to mention his tame bear Bessie whom he takes for walks round Chelsea.'

'Are animals his line?'

'Only the human variety: the scurviest, most devious sort you can imagine. I am engaged on a little business with him at the moment - very hush, hush. Cannot really say anymore about it!'

Just past the Patisserie Valerie on Old Compton Street the cabbie took a left, and the Wolseley engine chugged up Dean Street. Turning into the narrow alley that emerged second on the left, they pulled up beside an imposing white building. Vicky reached for his pocket book, but Crowley forestalled him and to the surprise of his former acolyte - who was, nevertheless, relieved at this evidence of solvency - produced a large white note from his own wallet and handed it to the driver. 'Gorblimey! I can't change this,' the latter said in a tone that implied it should be made a criminal offence that he was even asked to. With a regretful air, Crowley took it back, permitting Vicky to glimpse the stark black writing in which the Bank of England promised to pay the bearer a hundred pounds. The Beast had been in possession of the note for the last three years. The inability of anyone to change it meant he had so far saved three times its value. Vickybird removed a more modest florin from his pocket, which covered the fare, leaving three pence for a tip.

The printing works on the ground floor adjoined a narrow entrance, which admitted them into a short passage. At the end of this was a lift, which creaked alarmingly as it deposited them in a reception hall on the third floor. A uniformed flunkey approached, who relieved Crowley of his top hat, case and cane, Vicky of nothing, and led them to a plinth, on which rested a visitor's book which the Beast took some five minutes to fill with a plethora of titles. Then the flunkey ushered them through a hall lined with nudes by Matisse into a room the width of the building, which boasted a long mahogany bar. At the suggestion of the French painter, every inch of the walls as well as the coffered ceiling had been covered with squares of glass cut from the looking glasses of an eighteenth-century chateau. These mirrored tiles endowed the drinkers who sat at the bar with a second, more exotic existence as their reflections were distorted into the faces of gargoyles.

'A good place for crystal men,' Crowley muttered taking Vicky by the arm and guiding him to the bar. A few glances were cast in their direction, but in general, it seemed the entrance of the Beast with his companion struck the crowd, some in bow ties and tails, and others in more bohemian polo necks and corduroys, as unremarkable. Founded by David Tennant, with Augustus John as president, the Gargoyle had been intended to bring together artists and the upper crust. Though himself neither, Crowley, paradoxically, fitted both descriptions.

'A little late for wine,' he said surveying the amazing variety of bottles ranked along the shelves. 'Give me Strongwater!'

The barman glided away and returned with a pale bottle labelled 'Alcool de Mont Angel', a drink much favoured in the eighteenth century due to its ability to induce vomiting. More cautiously, Vicky ordered red wine and paid the not exorbitant, given the time and the location, three shillings. Snatches of conversation drifted to him. Nearby, one intense looking man demanded of another, 'Heathenise me with your Marxist-Leninism if you must;' while the cut glass voice of a woman declaring sex passé floated from a banquette. A creature in a velvet jacket and canary-yellow waistcoat, with a cruel, pampered face, bemoaned the ice that for some reason unknown to Vicky, who was himself severely discomfited by the heat, had entered his heart. This was not your usual nightclub banter.

'Still dancing?' asked Crowley.

'Trench fever ruined my co-ordination,' Vicky explained.

'Pity! You were astonishing.'

Vicky followed the Beast across the room and descended the gold and silver staircase, feeling like a bird of paradise as, matching his steps, his reflection merged into the lines of an infinite rainbow. They stepped onto the floor of a large L-shaped room, at the foot of which were the band and cockpit-sized dance floor, the rest of the area being occupied by tables, red plush-covered chairs and banquettes. Like the bar, this area was still crowded, though there was only one dancer on the dance floor. He was a flamboyant individual who had improvised a solitary Apache dance, which had involved the removal of most of his outer garments, and with its flailing movements, had effectively barred the space to anyone else.

The Beast moved forward until they reached a table, whose cloth, already boasting several stains and one broken glass, draped onto the knees of Dylan and the Spectre jittering in time to Missouri Moon. Absence had done nothing to improve the condition of either, Vicky noted, as the dumb show of horror on the Welshman's face slowly gave way to an equally hideous grin.

'Delia, what an unexpected delight!' exclaimed the Beast, surprising neither Dylan nor Vicky, both by now accustomed to the breadth of her acquaintance. He heaved his bulk onto one of the two vacant chairs and indicated his companion should take the other. Dylan spluttered an objection.

'So I find my artist friend once more,' continued Crowley gleefully, 'exploring the facets of this crystal realm.'

'There is a flaw in the glass,' came the Spectre's doom-laden tones. 'The palace will burn before the Crystal Night. They shall smash all the shop windows in Jewish Bermondsey.'

Seeming to find this observation particularly arousing, the Beast half-rose, leant forward and pausing long enough to admire the Spectre's cleavage, grasped her right arm and brought it to his lips. He planted a kiss on the tree of blue veins where they ended at the wrist, opened his mouth, then seeming to think better of it, reluctantly released the flesh. His fingers slid into the inside of his mouth and began irritably to jiggle his left incisor. It was his serpent's tooth; honed to pierce just such promiscuous surfaces as that of the Spectre. The tooth was loose and would finally forsake its master in the year to come. His tone was tetchy when he next addressed her: 'Why is it, Delia, that one takes cocaine gluttonously, dose upon dose, neither feeling the need for it nor having any damned idea why one's doing it?'

'I say, did someone mention cocaine?'

The wind billowing in the sail-like plus fours of a man passing their table had briefly ceased. The Monk, lately of the Wheatsheaf, stared down at them. In tow was the Chick.

'We're looking for Brilliant Chang,' chirped the latter. 'We want to buy some grass.' A look of doubt flushed his scrubbed features.

'Does it make you...' he hesitated, '...full of fun? I mean does it make you want to do things.' A blush sidled up his cheeks and his voice grew sly: 'Larks!'

'Larks!' repeated Dylan in disgust.

'Hashish is the drug which loosens the girders of the soul but is in itself neither good nor bad,' responded Crowley. 'It saved my life on one occasion.'

'You sound like you know about such things,' said the Monk.

'I have trudged hundreds of miles without a rope over snow-covered glaciers and nobody has ever attempted to repeat my major climbs on Beachy Head. I may add a little grimly that the same remark applies to my excursions into the uncharted depths of the mind. However, please won't you join us?'

Crowley had appropriated the table just as he hoped to appropriate these likely looking youths.

'Boys!' a voice rang out. 'Don't even think of it!'

A woman swathed in tiger fur had pushed herself to the forefront. It was Betty May.

'So you met your maker,' she hissed at Vicky, 'just as Raoul did to his eternal cost.'

Crowley seemed unphased by the onslaught. 'I but lit the fuse. Is it my fault he could not stand the blast? Besides, he was Adonis. He had to re-enact the myth. You never understood that, did you?'

'You are the thief what stole my letters!'

'Certain ravings of yours did come into my possession,' admitted Crowley, who had used them in the case he brought against Nina Hamnett. 'They resulted in a fine of fifty guineas I did not possess; an outrageous figure - way beyond the literary merit of the articles in question.'

The Monk and the Chick chortled in unison. Betty May extinguished this with a glare.

'There are things about you I'd rather die than let anyone know. Acts so vile that even to invent a name for them would forever soil the language.'

'You flatter me, Betty. If I have been guilty of anything, it is only to have enlarged the fundamental basis of my philosophy. Uprightness and penetration are the essential prerequisites of such a quest. No deed but we dared it, boys!'

The varsity men tittered. Betty May silenced them with a frown.

'He'll have you wrapped in his coils as quick as you can say the moon is black. Just look at that sad shade beside him.'

'Must we really endure these yellow press clichés,' moaned Crowley. 'Yes, I say unto my accusers, only he can be truly happy who has desired the unattainable. Why, in great matters it is enough merely to have had the intention. What if I transcended this wrinkled drop wasted by a God: and if the means I used to do so proved odious to the men of straw who publish newspapers and the half-wits who read them, a further so what! There are many portals that open onto Samadhi, but I have always opted for the quickest route.'

'I say!' said the Monk.

Crowley appraised him with the meticulousness of connoisseur. With the sprightliest of movements, he rose and tapped the student on his left shoulder. 'A monkey in Ceylon bit your mother on the same spot last year. The infection did not prove fatal.'

'God, yes! How could you possibly know?'

'Because in the places I could take you to - and you very much have the look of someone who could benefit from such a voyage - reside certain powers and formulations of the mind that allow one to cross centuries from one's armchair and voyage through interstellar space at one's desk. The poet sitting opposite, for example, will die, surprisingly enough, not from the effects of the drink he drains with the avidness of a calf, but from a drug. I know such things because I am dealing in the innermost secrets that are more than life eternal and shine brighter even than the undying flame in the Temple of Thoth. Would you stand shoulder to shoulder with me on the threshold of the Aeon, of which I am the harbinger? Such an outstretched hand was offered, I believe, by Jesus to the fishermen. Have you an income?'

'My father...'

'Would never hear of you having anything to do with a man such as he!' cut in Betty May. 'Now be a darling and take me in your arms. I'm longing to tango.'

So saying she tugged the reluctant Monk away, and wheeling him around, strutted onto the dance floor in time to the tango being beaten out by Alexander's Band. Carried in their train, the Chick brooded on the sidelines.

'Tiresome slut,' muttered Crowley.

'Aren't they all,' sighed Dylan, 'with their frills, mascara and convoluted curtsies. I've had them up to my eyeballs.'

'An unsanitary feat,' observed Crowley. 'I say nothing less will do than congress with over a thousand women, drawn preferably from eighty to ninety races, if one wishes to know about the sex in sex.'

'I'm your man! Last night there was the greasy Pole and a couple of weeks ago I was trawling up the Danube. Of course, I much prefer the Liffey. Just think! Two pert Irish cherries and flanks like milk squandered on that ram-red goat King John. A Jubilee Bond of an adjective, eh,"ram" for "red"? Saw it in a dictionary, used it in a poem and now I cannot find it again. There should be a Pinkerton's for poets.

"Excuse me, Detective, could you find my word?" But you know what the trouble is? At the very time when boys are green and girls are red, at the howling onset of puberty, they are left to mould like cheese till their twenties when it's up to them find out what it's all about. It should be, "Ah, good evening, Mrs Jenkins, I've brought my Glynis round to play with your little Tom. She is all of thirteen and just burstin' for it. I'll fetch her in the morning."'

'Yes, Sir,' boomed Crowley, 'the church, the chapel and the registry office all must go. Personally, I shall not rest till sodomy is recognised as every Englishman's birthright.'

Dylan launched into a protracted burst of coughing that almost finished him. When he came out of it, he was white-faced and meek. 'What drug will kill me?'

'Morphine,' said Crowley.

'Horrid stuff!' said the Spectre with a sniffle.

The Beast seemed angry at having tendered such privileged information.

'Our youngling is a poet,' put in Vicky; 'a very fine one.'

'Forgive me! I did not realise we had a son of Orpheus on board. Are you one of those pencil sharpeners who twitter on about the mundane dilemmas of suburban man, an ape that gibbers on the other face of Thoth? Or are you a true child of the muses, vibrating at the frequency where art becomes magick and has the power to give gods form?'

The Beast had strayed onto that one patch of Dylan's earth not buffeted by drunken winds of slapstick and pastiche. Almost involuntarily, a stream of words rumbled from him, which conveyed to his listeners the molten lyric of Light Breaks Where No Sun Shines.

'Where no seed stirs, the fruit of man unwrinkles in the stars,' repeated Crowley when it was over. 'A singularly occult observation, though not one of course that would be subscribed to by my school. I have always observed that nine times out of ten the true British pagan is a Norman or a Celt. You, Sir, are a Bard. Now you shall hear me!' So saying he recited his own City of God – finally, Dylan was condemned to hear it all.

'Exquisite!' exclaimed Vicky.

'Many have remarked on the strange coincidence that Leamington in Warwickshire should furnish England with her two greatest poets - for one must not forget Shakespeare. I can see the majesty of it carried our poet away. I shan't turn him into a toad after all.'

Dylan, who took such threats seriously, turned his haggard features in the direction of the dance floor. The challenging gaze of the velvet-jacketed man Vicky had noticed upstairs met him. The creature waltzed over and declared in a tone of outraged camp, 'Your tumbling coif, my dear! So greenery-yallery!'

The poet rose, grabbed a passing waiter and propelled him onto the dance floor.

'Hardly your type, Delia, I would have thought,' observed Crowley.

'He's a nice boy.'

'Always thought you preferred rock to putty.'

Vicky gazed across at the band that had just launched into Let's All Go to Mary's House. Wine and the glamorous surroundings sparked once more the illusion that his life had returned to more illustrious pathways than those he was accustomed to exploring with Runia in Boundary Road. In his patched and threadbare jacket, hair unkempt and tie askew, he in reality cut a ridiculous figure. It was a pressure in the loins, however, not a desire to restore a semblance of sartorial order, which prompted him to rise and foppishly cross the floor in the direction of the toilets.

'You may not be ahead, but you could still quit,' a husky voice hooked him at their threshold.

The pert woman did nothing to bridle his eyes as they strayed from the delicate bones at the base of her neck to a bust that rose like Zeppelins, he thought absurdly. Almost with shame Vicky realised he desired her. Any such feelings he had nurtured for Runia, faint stirrings sparked by their endless twittering about Lawrence and the 'progressive thing', while her sick husband, the painter, tossed in a loveless bed, had been soon dispelled. Elopement had taught him she was one of those curiosities so terrified by sex she praised its every avatar. Then there had been his dark-eyed wife, Kathleen. At the outset, her caresses had invoked Pan, but as habit and domestic rectitude insinuated itself, he had softened and wrinkled, and she had absconded for the weekend with a travelling salesman. He was left cheerfully waving goodbye in the Sussex sunshine, then, a few moments later, heartily greeting the vicar's purse-lipped wife as she trotted stiffly by, oddly proud of his horns. Contemplating Betty May was like being invited on a voyage; and it was so long since Vicky had even had a day trip that he wondered at this urge to travel.

'You wouldn't understand,' he told her. 'Unfinished business...'

Nearby, there was an eruption of nasal voices with grating edges. Impelled recently by shaky finances, David Tennant had opened up the club to visitors from Chiswick and Wimbledon who wanted an after theatre supper. The regulars disdainfully referred to such people as "the dentists", and one such couple, sitting at a table a few yards away, were squealing in horror. A scruffy individual had just snatched their bottle of claret from the table, and in a mad pastiche of aristocratic drinking habits, was pouring its contents into the shoe he had removed. The dark brown brothel-creeper boasted a large hole in the sole, which as Dylan raised it to his lips rained wine down onto his shirtfront.

'Isn't he a darling!' purred Betty.

The Gargoyle was a liberal place, but there were limits. By the time Vicky had returned from the toilet he saw Dylan engaged in an intense discussion with a tall man with a tragic face. The Welshman, who seemed in the mood for disrobing, suddenly tugged up his shirt to reveal fair and blameless skin, not the seaman's sweater this same David Tennant had lent him at the beginning of the month. As Vicky reached his table, the Welshman was being escorted off the premises with his flagship the Spectre. He was bound for a port where he would pick up the tainted cargo that would so embarrass resumption of trade with Caitlin.

Dylan's exit signalled a more general exodus, which included Betty May with her eager charges. Vicky glanced at his watch and saw it was five past two. At a quarter past, Alexander's Band halted midway through No Foolin and struck up a march whose strident figures more normally crackled over the wireless at ten-thirty every night to mark the closedown of the B.B.C. Waiters froze, their glass-decked trays held in salute before them, while the seated rose, adopting stiff postures and a mask of duty, so at variance with the careless gaiety that had flushed their faces but a moment before.

Crowley's delicate hands darted to the back of his neck and undid the chain that bore the rose and cross, which he then placed in his top pocket. His face adopted a bulldoggish expression.

'The King and Queen,' he announced in an entirely altered voice, gruff and orotund, himself rising.

Gazing at the top of the stairs, Vicky saw that this pronouncement was astonishingly correct, at least in its first part, and the star struck in his nature went nova.

The dapper figure, with his delicate slim build, pale linen suit and two-toned shoes that clicked down the stairs with the panache of a tap-dancer, was immediately recognizable from a thousand Pathé newsreels. How often Vicky had seen him inspecting a mine in the impoverished Rhonda Valley or debonair in helmet and goggles in the cockpit of the Gypsy Moth he would take to Balmoral, the first monarch to fly. As Prince of Wales he had been the promoter of the Windsor knot, green alpine hats such as the one Vicky still regretted, suits in loud and glaring checks that had so appalled his father. Even as the yet uncrowned King, he was still the prince of youth; a wind blasting the fusty corridors of St. James, whose sympathies with the "German Experiment" alarmed Whitehall. Patently, this was Edward. However, the slim woman beside him of identical height, with the ironed down black hair, large nose and protruding jaw, was no queen Vicky had heard of - this despite the elegance of the shimmering dinner coat by Mainbocher that seemed, most appropriately, to be made of spun glass. He whispered as much to Crowley.

'As surely as the Angels rule the Aethyrs she reigns over him,' the Beast growled in his new voice. 'You, of course, a typical member of the British public, have never heard of her - she is the kingdom's best kept secret. The French know all about her and the Yanks. It will not be long until Beaverbrook or Rothermere decide to blazon the name Wallis Simpson across their grubby broadsheets. For he will not give her up; he is utterly bewitched. I speak as an authority.'

This was the second time that night Vicky had heard the name "Simpson". On the first occasion, it had been two sibilants briefly damming the glottal flow of Arabic. Now it acted like an incantation, summoning the man Vicky had seen in Crowley's room. There he was behind Wallis and Edward, smartly negotiating the glittering staircase. At its foot, he overtook the couple, and acknowledging with only the slightest irritated flicker of his left eyebrow Crowley's presence, strode manfully to an alcove, where a table was being immaculately set by two waiters. Then, as Vicky and Crowley straightened from their bows, the woman turned and glanced at the Beast.

Lowering himself onto a chair, Edward signalled to the band who broke off from the National Anthem. An infectious smile lit his boyish features as they launched into the upbeat strains of his current favourite, Ukulele Dream Girl.

Apart from the music, the room remained hushed. Even the sorcerer and his failed apprentice were silent. Faces cast anywhere but at the royal table longed to turn, and if for an impudent instant they did, they saw Wallis turn on the King, who was drumming his fingers on the table, his face in repose streaked with melancholy, and commence to nag him. The King blushed. His fingers moved nervously to the stem of his glass and lifted it, but in this they were censored by another barb from his consort. He listened, meekly, and then nodded. Victorious, Wallis revelled once more in the glances, while the King-Emperor, fêted as a god from Ceylon to Nyasaland, brightened like a schoolboy and downed the contents of his glass with all the enthusiasm of the heavy drinker. Vicky, who had travelled on the Astral, who had witnessed Gods and demons until such visitations seemed almost routine, found the scene incredible. Yet tritely came the thought, so irrelevant to the tragedy being played out before him, that this, out of all the day's anecdotes, would silence Runia.

Awe, however, was not a prerogative unique to him. The woman beside the King, with a face so blank it was like that of a player in a Noh drama, was equally humbled by her situation. It was to conceal this that her eyes, of such piercing blue that they would denote a colour, glacially monitored every motion of the besotted creature beside her.

Wallis was bored with the knitting, the bagpipe playing, and the private whine of a man the fates had given her as the ultimate foil imaginable to the deprivations she had suffered as an illegitimate child in Baltimore. To date he had furnished her with two hundred thousand pounds worth of jewellery and spent an extra ten thousand on silver fox furs imported from New York - but still she was bored. Because of this, and because she knew this little island, with its ridiculous pomp and beleaguered ruling class, would never accept her, she played the perilous game of reading the papers in the red dispatch boxes the King left so carelessly around Fort Belvedere.

She passed secrets to Von Ribbentrop on visits almost as frequent as the seventeen yellow roses that arrived from the German Embassy each morning. She dispatched invaluable insights into the thinking of the Cabinet to Count Ciano, Mussolini's foreign minister, who by one of those quirks that gives her story the aura of a Mata Hari, was a former lover. In return, she received priceless baubles bigger even than those given her by Edward. Inspired by self-abasement, the King turned a blind eye. Besides, half-German himself, he had been stirred by the ranting of the bohemian Corporal; a shoe-fetishist, he had thrilled at the crunch of the jackboots that his cousins, themselves high-ranking Nazi officials, strutted in. He was exasperated with the decrepit courtiers who moped over him, beneath clocks set half an hour forward to accommodate the grouse shoot - such creaking practices, so anachronistic when set beside the squalor of Jarrow. He had even toyed with the delusion of installing himself as the fascist God-King at the head of Mosley's government: or, less palatably, the President of a socialist republic. Either role, at least, would solve his problems concerning marriage.

Wallis's treason, however, had not gone unnoticed. Captain King was under express instructions to monitor the American. That his brief included contact with a man such as Crowley had been accepted with fortitude by MI5 who found themselves, not for the first time, underwriting the Beast's extravagances. They did, after all, regularly make use of other unusual resources such as Alexander Korda's "London Films" as well as a papal count, who was a director of Eno's Fruit Salts. That Wallis should now lean over and demand "that odd man who seems so familiar" be invited over was, however, not in the script at all. Captain King's mask of urbanity, whose very glue was the secrets it had grown so used to, cracked.

The King coughed: 'Surely you mean to do as Mrs. Simpson asks?'

'I am not certain that person is suitable for your majesty's acquaintance. He is a mountebank known to readers of the yellow press for certain unspeakable practices. His companion looks like a Jew!'

Wallis glared from their silky escort to the King: 'David, you're always saying how you want to mingle with the common folk. WE want to meet him!'

WE stood for Wallis and Edward and as such brooked no argument. Though this was one code he had not yet broken the

Captain rose, and crossing to the Beast's table, conveyed the invitation. Crowley, apparently unperturbed, removed a pungent Brazilian cheroot from his top pocket, stuck it into his mouth and thrusting out his chin pugnaciously, rose and loomed across to the alcove, with Vicky salaaming in tow.

At the table, Crowley bowed and greeted their "Royal Highnesses", admonishing them to "Do as thou wilt". Under the circumstances, this could not have been more appropriate. After the abdication, Churchill would describe the exiled Edward as a man who had done what he liked and now must like what he had done. The Beast then presented himself: 'Baphomet, Supreme and Holy King of Ireland, Iona, and all the Britains in the Sanctuary of the Gnosis, known to the vulgar as Sir Aleister Crowley.'

Wallis frowned. She could recall neither title nor name from Burke's Peerage, of which she was an avid reader.

'My knighthood was conferred on me in Spain by the Carlists,' the Beast explained.

'You do an awfully good imitation,' the King was gleeful. 'You've caught Winston to a tee.'

'Before there was Churchill, I am,' Crowley explained. 'Much the same could be said of Hitler.'

Captain King frowned and waved them onto two chairs the waiters brought up. The King, however, seemed intrigued. Ever over-attentive, he lit Crowley's cigar with a gold lighter, the hair, at forty as lush and gold as it had been at sixteen, flopping over his forehead. 'Very impressive chap that Austrian, eh!'

'I believe he is a reader of mine,' boasted Crowley.

'You're a writing sort of guy?' asked the man who had enquired of Thomas Hardy if he were the author of Jane Eyre.

'Words, Your Majesty, are but one string to my bow.'

'And the others?' cut in Wallis. There was more to the question than idle interest.

'I paint, Madam. I suppose you could call me an old master. However, the Book of the Law is by far my most important creation. The country that first adopts it will rule all nations. Let us hope Herr Hitler does not realize that first. I would be happy to furnish you with a copy. I will leave it at the reception. You will find it compelling, just as the German will discover much in it to concur with. He possesses, after all, every lineament of a magical regime: the symbol, the uniform, the gesture, why there is even a book, though not a patch on mine I am forced to admit. Frau Kûntzel, who translated and conveyed my work to the German Chancellor, is a follower of mine. I have many friends in Germany.'

'So have we,' said the King cheerfully.

Captain King stared at the tablecloth. Since cracking the Russian spy ring at the Woolwich Arsenal in the late Twenties, B5b, the division of MI5 he headed (so secret many in the Outfit would have been astounded had they known of its existence), had turned its attention to the threat from Germany. The fellow travellers of the Link and the Cliveden Set permeated the Establishment, even to its apex, as the King's words had just served depressingly to remind him.

'Only in Germany?' asked Wallis querulously.

Close to, the King diminished. Beneath his haunted blue eyes, premature pouches testified to insomnia and heavy drinking, while his skin was puckered and deeply lined by exposure to the colonial sun. Wallis, by contrast, possessed an alluring sheen, her skin bright and shell-like, her jet-black hair, clasped by an exquisite diamond clip, sleek as a geisha's. A man could almost want her.

'There are few lands that have not felt my tread,' the Beast conceded. 'Men of yellow, red, and brown skin have all stretched out their hands to me in friendship. I have prayed at Mecca, scaled the passes of Tibet. I even crossed China on foot!' There was a peculiar stress on "China" whose significance seemed apparent only to Wallis. She flicked her tongue around her mouth: a characteristic gesture betraying nervousness. 'It was in the winter of '24 I believe I glimpsed you, Madam, in the Field of Glittering Flowers.' He turned to the King. 'One of the purple mansions of Repulse Bay, Your Majesty, which specialise in the art of Fang Chu.'

'What a Swell name for a restaurant! Fangs Chew!' the King laughed, but was only echoed by Vicky.

No explanation of the term was forthcoming from Wallis, now frantically toying with her ruby and diamond bracelet. Instead, the Beast elaborated: 'Fang Chu is the art of producing such shivers of excitement the final gush of rapture can prove fatal.'

'Sounds a breeze!' said the King, cross-eyed with the strain of keeping up. A lover of Americanisms, his tongue had deserted his kingdom long before him.

Captain King stepped in, explaining in a slightly flustered tone that the Chinese Art was concerned with magical relationship in space, with rivers and the correct positioning of a goldfish bowl. Vicky knew that this form of eastern geomancy was in fact Feng Shui, but cowed by the company he stayed mum and wondered why Crowley did not correct the aide himself. The Beast might be mistaken in many things, but nobody could fault him regarding esoteric systems and their jargon.

'So that's why you moved everything round at the Fort,' said the King to Wallis. Then he cheerily rose, lifted the bottle, and to Vicky's utter astonishment, came over, brandishing it like a sceptre. There were gasps from the neighbouring tables. 'Let me wet your whistle,' he said, pouring the Krug into the glass, his hands weather-beaten and scaly from the long hours spent bill hooking the stagnant laurels round Fort Belvedere. There is a strain in magic, which cherishes bloodlines and the healing touch of Kings. However, a far more pedestrian awe filled Vicky. The King performed the same service for Crowley then returned to his chair, his eyes glued once more on Wallis.

'I could kill for a cigar,' he sighed.

'Your Royal Highness must have one of mine,' said Crowley, removing a cheroot from his top pocket.

'David only smokes Davidoff,' objected Wallis, unclasping her jewelled handbag in which she hoarded such treats. Thinking better of it, she slammed it shut.

'Madam, I see great bounty before you,' declared Crowley.

'Can you tell the future?' said Wallis.

'Indeed, the future tells me! An item will shortly come into your possession which will make the bracelet that adorns your lovely wrist, inscribed, I believe, with the touching words "Hold Tight", seem tawdry and fake.'

The effect of the Beast's prediction on Wallis was pronounced. She had grown visibly paler and in her agitation let the handbag fall onto the table. The phrase, which in itself constituted a kind of prophecy, really was the motto on the bracelet - a secret she had believed only David shared.

'The Oracle of Dawn is Brilliance, ring settled on the last five letters.'

'Go on!' she was eager, as though this was something she had been expecting to hear.

'The Time is Six Two Two. The Place, the Needle.'

Captain King stifled a groan. It was for him to give this information discreetly to Wallis. It was just as well, B5b were to be present at the handover. Crowley was far too loose a cannon to be left unmonitored at such a crucial juncture.

'I'm wretchedly tired,' Wallis murmured. 'Let's stay in town tonight. The Fort seems much too dismal.'

The King rose more quickly than she, Captain King a moment later. Wallis found the foot of the chair had caught the hem of her gown. The King crumpled to his knees and began to remove it.

'Well, that's the most extraordinary performance I've ever seen,' snapped his intended.

Her target reddened, and then stammered, 'You have made me feel so terribly badly. I know I am hopelessly spoilt and therefore horridly thoughtless. I'm so grateful to you for showing me myself.'

It was not the sheer abnegation of the King-Emperor that struck Vicky; the parallel he drew was much closer to home. Edward had his Vampire and he had his - the portly man lolling beside him, contentedly puffing on his cheroot.

VIII°
The Forty-Three

With windows open, the city slept beneath a star-filled sky. Clerks and shop girls snored in Surbiton, while under the arches of Waterloo Bridge, the gentlemen of the road savoured a night designed for sleeping outside. Slinking down a now deserted Dean Street, however, were the Laurel-and-Hardy like forms of Crowley and Vicky, the latter, improbably, the vessel of the God of War.

Mars was not just in him, however, it possessed the age. Many miles away, the insomniac Adolph Hitler was at his Eagle's Nest in Berchtesgaden gloating over Lady Houston's Saturday Review, which had petitioned Edward VIII to become a benevolent dictator. In North Africa, a diminutive general called Franco was plotting the coup that within a month would transform Spain into a vast bullring. Meanwhile in Rome, Il Duce planned the annexation of Albania. They schemed in concentrated cities. Even in sprawling London, however, the Genius of the Red Planet was brewing a war the appeasers fondly imagined they were averting by the very failure of nerve that would make it so terrible and its consequences so prolonged.

By now, Vicky was convinced Crowley possessed a covert purpose. The visit to the Gargoyle Club and palpable lack of surprise the Beast had displayed at the appearance of the King and Mrs. Simpson indicated that their steps were plotted as meticulously as the phases of a ritual. However, any enquiries he made on this score were met by a monosyllable from the pursed lips of the Wanderer of the Waste, who seemed absorbed in the intricate Cabbala of his thoughts as they crossed Shaftsbury Avenue and took the narrow passageway that led into Gerrard Street.

Soho was the true home of the nocturnal. There were drinking clubs, such as the Hambone and Tatty Bogle, the haunts of jazzmen, lesbians and toffs. Many of them operated on the fringes of the law, none more so than the club housed in the six-storey building they halted before, from which the strains of "Night and Day" padded softly to the pavement like a cat. This was the Forty-Three, which had become notorious a few years earlier for the war that the Home Secretary, known to a public flabbergasted by his killjoy energies as 'Jix', had waged against it, resulting in the exposure of a sergeant on the take and the imprisonment of its owner. The only other claim to fame of the establishment, to whose sturdy door Crowley now delivered a sharp rap, was that it had once housed Dryden. A spyhole opened, a latch turned, and they met the glare of a seedy-looking giant who wore the white silk tie, black shirt and two-toned shoes of the traditional spiv.

"'ave you a booked?' he demanded.

'Had a devilish time looking for change,' said Crowley who had taken the hundred-pound note from his wallet and was flourishing it under the bouncer's nose.

'Your mate ain't dressed.'

'I believe Brilliant Chang, currently in great agitation as to my whereabouts, does not stand on ceremony.'

'Say no more,' said the bouncer, squashing himself against the wall.

They mounted the narrow staircase, which ran steeply up two flights before admitting them into a large chandelier-lit room, with a band and singer at one end and a bar at the other. There were about fifty people dancing or sitting at the tables. The men were in tails, the women in evening skirts, which were lavishly trained and draped. Their duck-egg blue, pale green or scarlet testified to the impact the Chinese Exhibition was having. Others wore more lurid outfits, with a sprinkling of men gangster-suited like the villain who had admitted them. A large, silver-haired woman wearing a dress of Edwardian style, cluttered with innumerable strings of pearls, sailed to greet them. This was Mrs Conway, successor to the late lamented Mrs Meyrick, still languishing in Holloway for her services to pleasure.

'Lord Boleskine,' she murmured in an Irish lilt, 'your usual table?'

The Beast, trailed self-consciously by Vicky, permitted himself to be conducted to an alcove. A girl with bobbed blonde hair and vermillion lips brought champagne. Crowley ogled her as she snaked away, while his companion jiggled the little change remaining in his pocket and reflected on the futility of hundred-pound notes. Beside the bandstand, a sleek Chinaman, dressed immaculately in a sharp grey suit and pale silk tie, huddled in animated conversation with a pasty-faced hostess.

There was a commotion on the dance floor, prompted by the passage through the throng of a skinny woman who looked extremely drunk. Tilted on her head, at the same rakish angle as the pink beret Vicky had last seen her in, was a sailor's hat, which bore the words HMS Fitzroy on its band. The woman was tugging along the owner of the rest of this costume, a burly youth hardly out of his teens. The blood left her face when she spied Crowley; the Beast, by contrast, was effusive in his greetings and insisted she join them.

'Don't know if I should,' giggled Nina. 'You're such a wicked man.'

'Nonsense! I am "Little Sunshine" remember?'

He rose and helped the woman and her beau onto two chairs.

'So you found him.' exclaimed Nina, peering at Vicky. 'You were like a train this afternoon; anyone could tell you were chugging to Crawley.' The laughter inspired by this execrable joke she celebrated in solitude. 'What fun we've been having! Super party at Byron's. Lashings of champagne! Must have drunk gallons of the muck, my deahs.'

'Do have some more,' insisted the Beast, filling two extra glasses the waitress had brought.

'And I met Bert,' twittered Nina. 'Isn't he wonderful?' She squeezed the sailor's arm. 'His ship really is called the Fitzroy. It took Darwin to the Galapagos just to prove that we are all monkeys, can you imagine? I told him I am in the V & A with me left tit knocked off, but he will not believe me. I think I'll sue.'

'An activity you've grown rather adept at of late,' said Crowley with just the barest trace of acid.

'Time before last I got a hundred and fifty quid from the Daily Mail after the imbeciles said I'd been present at one of those ceremonies the King of Redonda inflicts on us all.'

'I'm the Wizard of the Isle,' said the Beast, 'which is apt when you consider the elements of Prospero in my nature.'

'Well, Dylan's the Bard and 'Gus John's the bloody Court Painter. Anyway, in March I had another bit of luck. One of the rags published a photo of Betty May and said it was me. I dashed round and got five white ones out of them; a couple of hours later Betty did the same.'

'How fortunate are the women of my acquaintance,' said Crowley drily.

'I only said they were rumours about the missing babies in Sicily. That was nothing to the libels John Bull printed. You could have made stacks!'

'I do on occasion find it expedient to turn the other cheek. Wouldn't you agree, Albert?'

'Eh?' said the sailor.

'Cheeks? Don't you like to turn them?'

'Oh, Crow,' giggled Nina. 'If you flirt with my Bertie, I might get quite shirty and do something dirty.'

This time Vicky, more parrot than parakeet, joined her in laughter.

'You should get out more,' Nina advised him. 'It suits you.'

'The King was at the Gargoyle,' said Vickybird, who could still hardly believe it himself.

'Was he with that dreadful American woman? I bumped into them myself at Mrs Cavendish's hotel. She treated him like a servant. Can't imagine what he sees in her.'

Crowley as ever was keen to offer enlightenment. 'She is versed in a certain art practised in China that can arouse the most moribund of men; a technique that involves the application of hot oil and a prolonged and carefully modulated massage of the entire torso. It is called Fang Chu.'

'Sounds heavenly!' said Nina. 'But how do you know?'

'She was one of the line up in a brothel in Hong Kong I visited. Besides, there is a dossier on the subject some friends of mine made up, which also detailed another of her activities not entirely unfamiliar to our friend over there.'

By the bandstand, the Chinaman was scrutinising them like a basilisk.

'I've always wondered about these "friends" of yours, Crow. I mean you've done some pretty rum things, but you've never been nabbed - at least not in this country!'

Over the last thirty years, the Beast had been accused of sodomy, drug taking and the ritual murder of infants, in court as well in the press - activities the merest whisper of which would have brought ruin to any other man. Yet rather than deny such accusations he had flaunted them, even confessing to the last crime in print - though he had in fact been employing a metaphor for the sacrifice of semen. What could explain the mysterious refusal of those in high places to prosecute him? The Beast, it seemed, would furnish no key. He sat there smugly like a sphinx.

None the wiser, Nina latched onto another topic, one that her lips had broached a thousand times before: 'I hope you boys have got some money because I'm wretchedly skint and Bertie hasn't got a ship's biscuit on him.'

'I do not mind telling you,' purred Crowley with an affability that struck Vicky as sinister, 'that you have encountered me at a most propitious moment. While it would be premature to say I am in possession of the readies, the fact is my rendezvous with riches is only a few hours away.'

'Oh Crow, I remember you in just such a vein in Paris all those years ago. Then, if memory serves, you had actually invoked the god of filthy lucre and his bounty was to be lavished at any sec'. You still owe me for the absinthe.'

This did not seem to be one of Crowley's more cherished memories.

'On that occasion, if I am not mistaken,' he said with a glare that made Vicky cringe, 'I was badly let down by a friend who absconded from the Work in order to spend his inheritance exclusively on himself: the money, moreover, was entirely the result of our very strenuous Invocation of Jupiter. Theft is not too blunt a word! I must add that he paid a terrible price. However, enough of that! Man's life is buffeted from wave to wave, sometimes in the ebb, sometimes in the flow, and I am ascending with dizzying speed to a crest. Waitress!'

Any waitress in earshot was deafened by the band's strident version of Big Chief De Sota and the cowboy whoops the singer's Al Bowlly-like rendition was exciting from the audience. The Chinaman sauntered over, dapper and cat-like. Close to, however, he lost something of his charm for small acne scars pitted his oily cheeks. Vicky put him in his mid-forties.

'Permit me, Prince Choia Khan,' he said in a voice of gravel with silky borders.

'Prince Choice Can!' repeated Nina.

'An honour conferred by the Emperor at the Ceremony of the Serpent, Peking, nineteen hundred and six,' Crowley tersely explained.

One snap of the Chinaman's immaculately manicured fingers summoned a waitress.

'Krug!' he announced. 'Put that also on the tab.' He indicated the Bollinger with a dismissive wave.

'You see,' Crowley was gleeful. 'It is hardly appropriate that the Greatest Living Englishman should skulk through this foggy metropolis like a thirty-bob-a week pen pusher. With some pride, I may say that I have borne with equanimity the poverty proper to an artist. I took an oath never to benefit from my writing, and apart from Diary of a Drug Fiend, whose success was entirely the fault of my publisher, the British public has been stalwart in ignoring me. Men of another race discern my genius. Brilliant Chang, may cherry blossom rain upon your house.'

The band had slowed the tempo. Stepping to the mike the singer, who possessed Al Bowlly's swarthiness but not a shiver of his voice, launched into Noel Coward's Twentieth Century Blues.

"In this strange illusion, chaos and confusion,
People seem to lose their way.
What is there to strive for?
Love or keep alive for?"

'Pity Al's in New York and not here to do it properly,' sighed Nina. 'That's his Ex over there, the pale streak dancing with that pink-nosed toff. She's got eyes like pinholes and a left arm like a pincushion.'

Several couples on the dance floor were smooching, including the portly gentleman just referred to, who was in fact the mayor of Basingstoke. In one arm, he was clutching a giant panda he had just purchased from the platinum-blonde hostess whose neck he was licking - an equally costly kangaroo and a koala bear already awaited him in the cloakroom. The hostess released her partner and with an agitated frown padded over in their direction. Skinny, with nervous eyes and a sickly complexion caked by powder, she resembled a once fine building fast approaching ruin. She went directly to the Chinaman and hissed something in his ear. Chang's only reaction was to take a deep drag on his cigarette.

'I can pay you tomorrow,' she implored, this time more audibly. 'Just a pinch to take away the jags.'

She grasped his wrist and her nails dug into it, forming welts in the hairless, sallow skin.

'Go home,' he said. 'Sleep it off. Tomorrow you feel better.'

A couple of the bouncers were elbowing their way through the dancers. The woman looked frantically around. Her eyes fell on Crowley.

'What's in the case?' she demanded.

'Bats' wings, mandrake and the skin of toads curdled in the blood of newt. Would you like to see?'

'You're that witch fellow, aren't you?'

'I am not a which, Madam. I am a who!'

This stunned her for a moment. The singer's voice drifted over, neatly encapsulating her predicament.

> "Say hey! Hey!
> Call it a day!
> Blues,
> Nothing to win or lose,
> It's getting me down.
> Who's escaped those dreary
> Twentieth Century Blues!"

She refocused on Chang, releasing his wrist in order to fumble in the moiré handbag slung over her shoulder.

'If I can't have any, no-one else gets it either,' she screamed, producing a derringer as silver as the bag.

So fast that Vicky saw no movement, only the issue, Chang grabbed her wrist and forced it upwards. The gun went off, the bullet embedding itself in the ceiling. The bouncers were now on the woman, one of them seizing the gun. In a cacophony of cymbals and wrong notes the band crashed to a halt, taking the dancers with them, but not the police who were pouring in through the fire escape. The raid had been planned several days before and had nothing to do with the shooting - but they had heard the report. Led by a tall detective in a mackintosh they forced their way through to the table, too late to notice the bouncer drop the gun onto the floor and kick it under the table.

'Who's been shooting?' demanded the detective.

'That is your weapon.' Chang indicated the champagne.

The detective, who was in his thirties and exceedingly handsome, peered dubiously at the bottle then the girl, 'What's wrong with her?' he said.

The two heavies released their captive, their brutish faces sporting the same blank look as hers.

'She's a good girl.' explained Chang. 'Very tired. Needs rest.'

'Are you up to your old dodges again, Bill?'

Chang spread his hands, a picture of innocence. 'You know me, Andy. I learn lesson - these days just simple restauranteur.'

'What about you others? Did no one hear a shot?'

A terrible abyss opened before Vicky. By nature, he was honest to the point of imbecility, and despite his anarchist youth, held authority in awe. His mouth sagged open, but simultaneously the Beast's claws dug into his knee, squeezing the truth out of him. Then Nina intervened.

'You're a dead ringer for Tyrone Power, you are. I'm going to dance with you.'

Extricating herself from the sailor, she sprang to her espadrilled feet, and seizing the detective - despite her slightness Nina's wiry arms possessed some power - tried to hustle him onto the dance floor. The sergeant and constables seemed too nonplussed to intervene. In an attempt to reassert some vestige of authority, the former examined the Beast, resplendent in his dress coat.

'And who might you be, Sunshine?' he demanded.

'Exactly that,' said Crowley reeling off a list of additional titles, including Patriarch of Isis and Sublime Knight of Kneph.

The sergeant blinked. Then, like the hostess before him, demanded to know the contents of the case.

'A little cocaine, a dead baby, and the climax of four thousand years of literature - a work that outstrips the Vedas and puts the Bible to shame!'

This seemed to open up an interesting line of enquiry, but then Nina, who was stroking the detective's arm, distracted them all again.

'Just feel those muscles! You should be a boxah.' So saying she lifted the trilby off his head and flung it onto the table. 'Dance with me!' she cooed.

'Christ Jesus!' he exclaimed, cueing his subordinates. Two of the burliest dragged Nina off and pinioned her to the wall.

'It's an utter disgrace,' the detective added, brushing his sleeves.

The sergeant agreed. 'It's not a place to visit, Sir.'

The appearance of the police had come as a mixed blessing to the guests as the club was licensed only till two, and it was now a few minutes after three. A distinguished silver-haired gentleman, who was in fact a Bishop, had thrust his glass of gin and bitters down the waistband of his trousers, where it spilt, spreading an embarrassing stain. He kept on beaming. Anything was better than the disgrace that would follow exposure in the press as an habitué of the 43. The ghastly shade of the Rector of Skiffley, recently devoured by a lion at the funfair where he made his living, still haunted the church. The police, however, seemed uninterested in the Bishop's ruse. They had abandoned the Beast's table and were rounding on Mrs Conway, whose infringement of the licensing laws was much more tangible.

'Most regrettable intrusion,' murmured the Chinaman. 'Can I not invite you to my establishment where refreshment soothe the nerves?'

Crowley rose with Vicky following. It seemed Nina was coming as well, for she nudged the sailor to get up. The Beast poked her hard in the stomach with his thumb, knocking her back onto the chair and said, 'Beware of railings, Nina!' a smile, which out of all the adjectives available, solely merited the description evil, puckering his jowls. The sailor bristled, but on Nina's pale face, there appeared a look of utter devotion. Following her gaze Vicky saw 'Gus John ambling past their table with two women in tow.

'Do what thou wilt shall be the whole of the Law,' declaimed the Beast.

'Well, I always do, you know. Hello, Crow, thought it was you. Hello, Nina. Hello, erhh...?'

Even a schwa from such illustrious lips fell like manna on Vicky's blushing ears.

'The Oracle of Dawn is Brilliance.'

'Yes, of course it is. Can't stop now. Must dash. Frightful rumpus, what!'

The first of the two women had a pert nose, blonde hair slashed into a fringe and almond-shaped eyes, but Brazil was stamped on her as surely as it was on her companion, Saliya, in a much sprucer state than when Vicky had seen her last. Sighting the Beast, she threw herself on him, flailing like a jellyfish. 'Alastor,' she moaned, 'I 'ave pray to all the Santos that you return. Take me to La Torre Eiffel and radish me.'

'Destiny, alas, has marked this night out for adventures of a less delectable nature,' said the Beast with dignity. 'Matters are afoot of which I can disclose nothing save that they will reap great dividends. I hope it is not asking too much of 'Gus if I entrust you to his care.'

'I've got Chiquita here,' said John, twirling his moustaches, 'and the doctors will go on about the strain to the old ticker. However, what the hell! The more the merrier I always say. Don't worry, Crow, I'll treat her like a daughter.'

'You are the father of your country, Augustus. By the way, I have a commission for you. I have decided the moment is propitious for a full portrait in oils.'

'Not the best time, I'm afraid. Just finished the portrait of that randy Taff who's been sniffing round my model. Lady Tweedsmuir will not leave me in peace until I have done hers. Had to put the fees up too, there's such a queue.'

'Money will not be of consequence.'

The painter stared at the Beast with bloodshot eyes. 'Well, glad to hear it, really I am. Can't stop now though. I will be in the Café tomorrow afternoon. We can discuss it when you collect Saliya.'

IX°
Shadows of a Shade

The establishment the Chinaman had invited them to was a small restaurant over the road from the Forty-Three. In 1936, there were only three Chinese restaurants in London, but Vicky, during his time at the Referee, had frequented the Shanghai in Denmark Street. The ducks skewered on hooks by the window, the tang of ginger, soy and black bean, the koi-filled fish tank, came as no novelty to him.

Conducted by Brilliant Chang, they crossed the tiled floor, so cramped it only permitted five tables, squeezed past the wok-laden cooker in the miniscule kitchen into an even tinier windowless room with a door leading out to a yard at the back. There were three stools and a low table on whose surface were a candle and a crumpled pack of cards. Chang flicked a grubby switch on the wall and the room was flooded with light. He barked something in Chinese. There was the sound of feet rattling heavily down the fire escape. The back door opened and a youngish man, whose features disappeared into puddles of fat, emerged. 'My nephew Loke,' said Chang.

While they seated themselves, the man waddled out into the kitchen and returned bearing a tray on which were three small tumblers and a bottle bearing a vile-looking green liquid with a lizard pickled in it. He set this down on the table and after filling the tumblers, went over to the shelf, opened a cedar wood box and removed a pipe and a round, ivory-inlaid box that he brought over. He lit the candle, which was made of ghee and gave off a fatty smell.

'Everything is proceeding satisfactorily,' purred the Beast, after downing the contents of the tumbler in one slug. 'Brother Neptunus has arrived in London. We cannot be too careful, however. He is sure to be watched, and besides....' The Beast owed his German follower a great deal of money and was delaying their reunion until a more propitious moment. 'The gift will, therefore, have to be collected and brought to the final rendezvous as arranged. The Oracle of Dawn is Brilliance. Our friends in Berlin are delighted.'

Espionage and magic, both of which thrived on shadow and the recondite, had co-existed down the centuries like Siamese twins. One had only to think of Enochian, the language of the angels, which Dee and Kelly had used to encrypt their work with the Elizabethan Secret Service. Crowley, Vicky realised, was speaking in code – but on whose behalf? Were the "friends in Berlin" persons who would be greeted by the enigmatic Captain King with a hearty handshake or was the Beast playing a double game?

'Please to try,' a sly voice dammed Vicky's stream of thought.

Loke was holding a tumbler out to him with a grin on his face that seemed indelible - but the eyes were cold and grey, devoid of any humour. Vicky took the vessel and brought it to his lips. He felt he was sipping from the cone of a volcano, as lava streamed down his throat, setting his guts on fire. He spluttered and spat the liquid onto the table.

'Victor's constitution is hardly robust,' explained Crowley, 'one of several factors, alas, that made him unfit for the Work.'

'You have Neptunus's address?' demanded Chang.

'That, unfortunately, is the one piece of the jigsaw that is still missing. What is the time, Victor?' Feeling like an accomplice, Vicky glanced at his watch. It was twenty to four. 'We should be furnished with that information within the hour.' Crowley did not elaborate on how this was to come about. 'Our reward shall not be in heaven,' he hissed instead.

'Why should it be?' responded Chang, with a sign to his nephew who opened the box and removed a pellet of dark resinous material which he began to pat round the pinhole of the pipe.

'Our Lady's Breath,' said the Beast, 'sacred to Jupiter as sovereign against pain and the gross integument in which the soul finds itself. Yet it is Mars who awaits us!'

Nevertheless, he took the pipe, and turning the bowl deftly, so it was but a hair's breadth from the candle flame, took a deep puff. Smoke spiralled upwards, pervading the room with an acrid aroma that reminded Vicky of liquorice. Crowley sucked three more drags into lungs so pulverized by ether, hashish and perique tobacco soaked in rum that the present infusion came as a bit of light relief. He returned the pipe to Chang's nephew who cleaned it with a knife and patted another pellet round the pinhole, this time offering it to Vicky. Though he had developed affection for the drug in Paris, Vickybird refused. He had an alarming vision of the police kicking the door down and pouring in. There they would find him, V.B. Neuburg, man of letters, smoking opium with men who might, be agents of a foreign power. However would he explain it to Runia?

'My friend is not a man of spirit,' declared Crowley with a smile.

'My nephew same, ' said Chang. 'I am man of lakes and rivers. Each day adventure. I do not care so much where I lay head. Loke dream only of return to Shanghai and safe, little restaurant he open.'

'It is indeed trying that men such as we must endure the trivial preoccupations of the herd,' agreed the Beast. 'I know the troubles you have had in that department...'

They sat in companionable silence for a moment, recalling the pariah-status Chang had attained some years before, almost rivalling that of the Wickedest Man in the World himself. This catalogue of notoriety had begun with an overdose of cocaine that had killed Billie Carleton, a celebrated Haymarket performer, on the morning after Armistice Day. It had then encompassed a legion of scandals involving trafficking and wild parties, with actresses and chorus girls trapped in a web of sex and drugs. Chang had operated out of the Palm Court Club in Gerrard Street. When this got too hot, he had moved to Limehouse, where his compatriots had loathed him as a westernised playboy. His eventual imprisonment had resulted in a wholesale drop in opium and cocaine arrests. On release, he had been deported and had passed into myth. He had been sighted in Marseilles, Port Said and China, where, it was alleged, he had become blind and impoverished. The most recent news had him in Antwerp, set to become the Dope Emperor of Europe. In fact, he had spent several years in Germany where he had forged his own links with the Abwehr. They had helped him re-enter Britain earlier that year. He did not intend to stay very long.

'Bah! It is fear of the unknown that makes people so scared of drugs,' the Beast went on. 'You have the yellow press with their unreasoning hysteria; the judiciary with their dread. There is a burning refusal to learn anything about them or face up to their implications.'

From the street came the sound of sharp rapping on the door. Vicky let out a tiny yelp. The others looked at him.

'The Address of Dawn,' declared the Beast.

Loke spluttered something. Crowley looked eagerly at him. The future lurked in the unlikeliest of places.

'16 Green Street, Mayfair.'

'The Prince is not referring to a nightclub dancer,' cut in Chang.

There came a louder rap. Loke hurried out and returned a few moments later followed by a tall man in a grey mackintosh.

'Gentlemen,' said Crowley. 'May I introduce our herald, a clarion also of high society, who you can call Tom.'

'Less of the high society, A.C.,' Driberg said in a tone so sonorous it sounded as if he was speaking in church. 'Personally, I can't wait for the tumbrels to carry Lady Cunard and her ilk to the hangman on Tower Hill!'

'Are you a Socialist?' asked Vicky eagerly.

'Of the lounge variety,' interjected Crowley. 'Actually, Tom occupies a more elevated position in the scheme of things. He is my magical heir. Let us hope he makes a better job of it than you did, Victor. The fact is, I am more than overdue a rebate of luck. Expelled first from Italy, then France because the gendarmerie believed my coffee percolator was a machine for making cocaine; declared bankrupt; banned by Oxford University from delivering my lecture on Gilles de Rais. What did they think I was going to do? Eat 800 undergraduates?' He looked at the gossip columnist and sniggered. 'Bet you could have done it, Tom.'

Brilliant Chang produced a slim gold case, opened it and offered Driberg a cigarette, which the columnist took and Loke lit with a chunky lighter. There was the smell of tobacco infused with something that reminded Vickybird of his schooldays and visits to the lab. Chang waved the case in his direction.

'I - hesitate - must refuse - most kind.'

'You sound just like Tom Eliot,' chuckled Driberg. He took a few drags, the contents of the cigarette seeming to perk him up. 'That exhibition really took the cake! Crazy stuff that Super-realism, eh? If bad, bogus and a bit twenties. Probably a dead-end. Alice meets Marx, and I mean the brothers.'

The telegraphic style of the Hickey column had infected Driberg's speech.

'Nothing I saw possessed the timeless quality of my own productions.'

'Were you there, A.C.?'

'Shall we say I went incognito?' The Beast's smirk strayed impishly from the columnist to Vickybird. 'The Surrealists are poking about in things they comprehend as little as a certain Frenchman's wife who tried to have her husband locked up in an asylum for his attempts to nail a shadow to a wall. Her name was Madame Daguerre. Shortly after, her spouse produced the world's first photograph! The parallel with my own endeavours is too obvious to need stating. A little demonstration might be in order.'

Reaching into the inside pocket of his dress coat he removed a fountain pen and began drawing on a napkin. What would appear wondered Vicky: a pair of vast buttocks? Dylan's face? Instead, the hurried strokes formed the outline of a pentacle. 'Tom, stare into the central space between the lines and tell me what you see!'

Driberg took a deep pull on the tainted cigarette, and leaning over the Beast, gazed down. 'Just the paper and the lines you've drawn, old man. No wait a moment, why...' His voice slipped off the coastal shelf of its usual register and in trance-like tones rose from fathoms deep. 'I can make out a small square volume, bound in red morocco and encased in baroque silver...'

'My magical diary from Cefalu,' gasped the Beast in amazement. 'I mislaid it in thirty-three. Dreadful year! Hardly surprising given the number. Go on, Tom! It is not for nothing I made you my successor.'

'There is writing, but I can't seem to read it. Perhaps something to oil the old waterway...?'

Chang clicked his fingers. His nephew went out to the kitchen and returned with another tumbler, which he filled with the lizard-infused liquor. The columnist took a deep swig, then in a dream-like murmur announced: 'The goat impregnates the Whore of the Stars. Her haunches writhe upon the Altar.'

'Yes! Yes! Except "her" should read "his" - purely figurative, of course. This is utterly incredible. He's making you look like an amateur, Victor!'

'Now this seems to be some kind of potion: "Smear it with tamarind fish paste. On this grill anchovies and sardines. Over this drip yolks of egg scrambled with cayenne."'

'My savoury fried bread! God, I never expected such a result.' Crowley seemed to be on the verge of hysterics. 'Tom, you are wasted on gossip. You could be the Nostradamus of Aeon. What else do you see?'

'Let me wet my whistle and I'll tell you.' Driberg took another glug then looked back at the drawing. 'No, it's fading. It's gone...'

The Beast began to cough violently. Vicky had never seen him so upset.

'Ravatory first floor. Up fire escape,' Loke said helpfully.

Crowley rose, slouched wheezing to the door, went out and could be heard puffing up the steps. Driberg leant back against the wall and began to chuckle. He is a truly wicked man, thought Vicky.

'There can't be many who have turned the tables on the Beast so effectively,' the columnist declared.

'How you know such things?' demanded Chang.

'Must have been the cigarette,' said Driberg.

In fact, not so long before a well-known circus illusionist called "the Great Cosmo", had got in touch with him and said he had acquired a trunk left at his landlady's in North London by Crowley, who had done a moonlight flit. Amongst the contents was the diary A.C. had kept in Sicily, from which Driberg had liberally quoted.

There was a muffled sound coming through the ceiling.

'Tom! Tom!' the Beast could be faintly made out bleating. Vickybird could not stop himself from asking why he had not been called. With relish the columnist rose, brushed past Loke, went out the back and nimbly mounted the rickety steps.

A peeling door on the left in the first-floor corridor demarcated the toilet. With its grimy washbasin and cracked mirror, it lacked, to Driberg's trained eye, the aplomb of the Victorian urinal in Rupert Street or the splendid art-deco affair opposite the Garrick - but a cottage was a cottage all the same. He entered with eager daintiness and found Crowley sniffling in the cubicle with his coat laid across his lap and his shirtsleeve rolled up. A leather thong bound the upper part of his arm but had proved an ineffective tourniquet. The Beast was holding a hypodermic, which he handed to Driberg with trembling fingers: 'I just can't find a vein.'

'Oh, is that what you wanted?' The columnist sounded disappointed.

'Be a good fellow,' Crowley wheezed, 'and see if there's one at the back.'

Squeamishly fondling the clammy skin, Driberg flipped the arm over and found a vein bulging out between the liver spots like a slug.

'I really don't think I'm up to this, A.C.'

'Come on, Tom. Gird yourself!'

After a moment's fumbling, the columnist inserted the needle, and with gaze averted, squeezed the plunger. The Beast's lids drooped and he leant back with nodding head. He had been habituated to heroin since the early Twenties, however, and soon a semblance of alertness had returned. 'Neptunus?'

'He called Fleet Street when I was filing my column.' Driberg told him and gave the address where the German was staying.

'Must be picking up the tab himself. The Abwehr could never afford it. Give the Chinks the address after I've gone.'

'Max won't stop pestering me. He's utterly besotted.'

'Indeed,' said Crowley. A brave sniper of heroin had penetrated his skull, granting a moment's reverie. 'Well, you are a charmer, Tom.'

'Who's the abject little man?'

'A toad-like Caliban called Victor Neuburg.'

'Didn't he drop you in it or something?'

'Rightly was he called "Brother I Shall Betray the Light!"'

'A.C. ...?'

What need had insinuated that husky note into his magical son's voice wondered Crowley. Driberg's eyes were pleading with his trousers. So that was it! Sometimes the attentions of his followers bordered on the impudent - but he was a doting parent. 'Go on then! If you must.'

With the grace of a prince of the church at prayer, Driberg knelt down in the cubicle. Would have been easier if I'd kept the kilt on, thought A.C., as the columnist began fumbling with his trouser buttons.

Of the scores of libidinous memories, he could have summoned at that moment, involving men, women and animals as well, those linked with a nineteen-year-old artist's model stole into his thoughts. How dexterous had been Fraulein Jaeger's poses! Pity she had killed herself the year before. Strangely enough, nearly all his Scarlet Women had committed suicide or turned to drink. He could not for the life of him imagine why. The memory of Hanni's delightful rump, which had been a welcome port in the stormy Berlin of the early Thirties, revived him and boded success for the current operation. However, there remained a problem. The degrees of sexual magick were clearly delineated: the Ninth, a self-pleasuring technique, also referred to as the Lesser Work of Sol, with which Amoun had engendered the universe; the Tenth, routine fornication; the Eleventh, buggery. Such oral favours as those Driberg was currently bestowing had yet to find a ranking. 'Ouch!' Now quite carried away, his magical son was getting a little rough. It had never occurred to the Beast before to classify fellatio as the Third Degree.

*

Vickybird was amusing himself by studying the contrast between Loke's face, which was as smooth as a blancmange, and Brilliant Chang's, so pitted it resembled the slopes of Etna. Sweat glossed the craters as chemical-smelling smoke streamed from the Chinaman's cigarette. He seemed full of bonhomie. 'I hope you are comfortable.'

'Actually, it's a bit close in here; thought I might nip outside for a bit of the fresh stuff.'

'But we have everything!' Chang's voice had been compared to liquid silk and had impressed several judges.

There was an old electric fan in a recess on the wall. His nephew went over, turned it on, returned beaming to the table and tipped what remained of the bottle into Vicky's tumbler. The cigarette case was thrust under his nose. He took one. With a grin wide enough to swallow lesser men, the nephew applied a flame to the tip. As he sucked, Vickybird wondered how cocaine had been packed into such a perfectly tailored cigarette - he had forgotten the ingenuity of Chinatown.

A sharp bullet of breath riveted his system. He was amongst the Angels of the Aethyrs. He was carried on the limitless wings of the imagination to a place he had not visited for many years. He became garrulous.

'Many thanks for your superb hospitality. May ducks rain upon your cherry blossom!'

Loke's grin yawned wider. His uncle indicated the tumbler as though not to drink it would bring the ceiling down on them: through the latter came a moan.

'I fear the Prince is ill,' said Chang. 'Man take pipe; pipe take pipe; pipe take man. Heroin is taking Mr Beast.'

Vicky thought this incredibly funny. He began to screech. The Chinamen seemed to find the racket hilarious. Loke slapped him on the back then thrust the tumbler into his hand. Vickybird gulped down more of the lizard juice and took a pull on the cigarette, which seemed to help the ingestion of the liquid. He repeated the experiment. Suddenly relating all this to Runia took on a different light. There he was with the biggest gangster in Chinatown, menace in every twitch of his finger, terror in each split second of his slanted eyes, laughing like a hyena. A tall, intense-looking man, whom he had once met with Crowley, would have thought it brilliant copy.

'Sax,' he said.

'You want see photo?' offered Loke.

Vicky explained he had meant Sax Rohmer, the author of the Fu Manchu series.

'Not a good man,' said Chang.

'Velly bad for business,' agreed Loke.

'He was a member of the Golden Dawn.'

'And we, the Trilaterals of Macau,' said Chang.

The Chinese did not shake with laughter. Laughter rippled through them like a wave.

Driberg had slunk back looking like the cat who had found the cream. 'A.C. needs a little more time to catch his breath,' he said, then addressed Vicky. 'I didn't realise who you were. Crow has told me such a lot about you.'

Vicky shuddered to think what.

'You raised Pan in the Sahara?'

'I was Pan,' Vickybird was surprised by his own assertiveness.

'Of course. Silly of me. '

'We raised many things.'

'I bet,' Driberg laughed. 'But you did see the devil in Paris?

'No, we conjured Jupiter and Mercury. In the desert, where we were the first since Dee and Kelly to make the Enochian calls, we evoked a demon - but it's best not to talk of that!'

'I'm a child of the muses myself. That is how I met A.C. when he came up to Oxford. Dame Sitwell has called me the greatest poet of my generation. I fear my promise will never be fulfilled, however. A bit like yours.'

Vicky winced.

'Journalism's hardening around me like a carapace,' continued Driberg. 'My old school chum Evelyn Waugh left the Express a few weeks before I joined. Had he stayed and become a news hawk we would never have had the novels. With me it's vice versa - well, at least the vice!' A look of hopelessness jarred with the unctuousness of the features. 'I should really run away: become a steward on a ship or something.'

Vicky understood this. He had often felt the same. Each thought himself so unique as he was guided by the Beast down the well-trodden path of poetry, magic and failure. What were Loveday, Driberg and he, after all, but shadows of a shade?

The back door had swung open and the latter rejoined them. 'The storm-fiend,' he sighed, lowering himself onto a stool. He used the name for the attacks of asthma that had assailed him since the ascent of Kanchenjunga. Loke offered Crowley the pipe but he waved it away. Driberg's turn was next.

'I think I've smoked enough for one day,' the columnist remarked blandly.

Vicky smiled his glutinous smile making him look remarkably like an orang-utan, considered Crowley. However could he have chosen such an abortion for the Work? He began to think of some more horrid things you could say about V.B.N., but opiates had mellowed him too much for such exertions. Instead, the faces of other acolytes welled up before him. The squat features of Norman Mudd; the clipped moustache of Captain Fuller, now a general, an expert on tank warfare, and one of only two British participants in Hitler's birthday celebrations the year before. In 1909, in the Star in the West, Fuller had proclaimed that it had taken the world more than a hundred million years to produce the now disgruntled conduit of these thoughts - the newborn Dionysus, Aleister Crowley.

After the spiritual crisis the Beast provoked, such relationships were invariably marked by rupture. When their wallets or their sanity was exhausted, he lost them. However, there were always others tantalised by an existence wreathed in mystery and the esoteric. It was a time when the old god was dead and Crowley seemed to be one of the few who knew the names of the new – (notwithstanding the fact that Ra and Horus had been worshipped three thousand years before). His ability to recruit such types from the two universities rivalled that of the Russian Secret Service. Eulogies were still in print concerning him, notably by Cammell and Stephenson. At the beginning of the year, Gerald Yorke, the most urbane and self-possessed of his followers, had handed him sixty guineas in La Tour Eiffel. There were aristocrats as well: blustering Lord Tredegar, with his MI5 connections, and Lady Frieda Harris, currently engaged on designing the Beast's Tarot, the pack of Thoth, under the charming alias of Jesus Chutney. Should he have used one of them as his go-between with Wallis? No, it was better to deal with her himself, he decided. It suited his sense of theatre. He admonished himself to concentrate on Mars, though all around was Jupiter.

A deep violet suffused the air. In the shapes conjured by the lamps he glimpsed the features of Amoun and Brahma, two of the mightiest of gods. His breast heaved with deliverance from strife; but of course, how when he was so close to the attainment of earthly riches could he be expected to shun such a Jupiterean glow? He regretted the Work he must perform. Four should be the number of this night not

Five. Nevertheless, was it not, after all, the very wiles of Bartzabel that would furnish him with bounty? How opportune it was that Vicky's reappearance had provided a new link to the gods. Mars was displacing Jupiter, and if you had the right type of vision, it was not hard to see the monstrous shadow the "Warrior Lord of the Forties" was casting before him. But then what? After the conflagration that would inevitably overtake the next decade? The view grew dim, its unique landmark that puzzling reference to the cowed and abased Eighties in the Book of the Law. Did that mean that by then universal peace would be assured to everyone, at least until the ending of the millennium? He must get Victor to interrogate the Spirit on this score. Despite colossal failings, there was part of Vicky's psyche that was naturally attuned to the astral. He was an excellent channel and the Beast was eager to scry. Had not a former evocation furnished news of the disaster about to detonate the Balkans and the deluge of the Somme?

He blinked. They were outside. The air was cool. The moon, as though disbelieving such a night could fall on London, curved above the rooftops like a scimitar. Borne upon the opium's velvet cushion they had left the restaurant, Crowley realised, and were just emerging into Charing Cross Road. Opposite was a bookshop whose owner the previous winter had offered a derisory ten shillings for a grimoire the impecunious Beast had been trying to unload. He applied his Will and all the volumes vanished from the shelves. A similar exertion and glistening rows of the Equinox of the Gods replaced them.

Pleased by such trivial conjuring Crowley contemplated their next move. A billboard recommended lunch at Lyons. He made a hasty tally of the letters. 418 - The number of the Great Work! Footsteps disturbed this startling correspondence. In stilettos, fishnet stockings and tight red dress a prostitute was strutting down the opposite pavement. She pouted at them; mouth like a pomegranate; a come-on wink from one painted eye. Deep within him the Beast roared. He would do things to this Whore of the Stars she had never dreamt of. Yet no corresponding sap rose. There was a flaccidness in his pants, which in recent months had become worryingly the norm. Driberg had been a chore, and even the operation in La Tour Eiffel with Saliya had been flimsy, staged more for Vicky than out of any genuine desire. The raging sea was dwindling to a millpond.

'Have you change for a cab?' he demanded.

Reduced to nine pence, the price of fifteen fags, Vicky shook his head.

'Then we shall walk,' decided Crowley. 'Did we not after all cross Spain on foot to say nothing of the Sahara, where I shaved your head, leaving only two tufts of hair, twisted into horns and dyed red, and introduced you to the Bedouin as a captured Jinn?'

Preferring not to dwell on this, Vickybird wondered where their steps were heading and if their rendezvous was to be with a being as terrible as that which they had encountered in the desert. He only, however, formulated the first part of this enquiry into words.

'To the river we go,' replied Crowley, who seeming sensitive to the subtext, went on: 'Though the Spirit that inhabits you pertains to the baleful sphere of Choronzon, the accursed and terrible demon we summoned at Bou Saada, Bartzabel is not so immersed in the world of adjectives. He still has a few nouns and a preposition or two at his disposal. There will be gibberish, but the age is infested with him; the acclaim of millions grants him eloquence. Life like society swings between the clemency of Jupiter and the severity of Mars. The Twenties were slack, money flowed, and justice was soft and apologetic. Then came the crash and the fomenting of a different spirit that is now maturing. Soon weakness will be crushed; the unfit and the underdog will be trampled underfoot; events more terrible than any you or I could possibly imagine will seem routine. All this under the aegis of the Spirit we must evoke.'

A street dissected Charing Cross Road. On its south-eastern corner Leicester Square underground station was closed but would, Vicky realised, be open in about two hours. Though there was no traffic, his feet hedged at the curb.

'There's no way out, you know,' insisted Crowley. 'Not for the age or you. If you come with me, you will be free of it. Society, on the other hand, has perhaps thirty more years until the pendulum swings back and the King dismounts from his Chariot and resumes his Throne. A brief lull, of course, before the ascension of Horus who will abolish the pendulum, the nation, the family and usher in the Aeon, in which the individual shall reign supreme.'

Still Vicky's scuffed shoes hesitated on the unlikely Rubicon of Cranbourn Street.

'You never understand, do you? The integrity of the Tree of Life hinges on the fact that each branch contains its own opposite. In your case a Flaming One of Mars, has made of you its habitation. Valour, severity, all martial virtues are notable by their absence. You cannot even cross the road!'

'I thought I had put such things behind me.'

'You thought you could forget magick, but it certainly hasn't forgotten you. You just took to hiding, a petrified rabbit trembling in a hole! Even when I came to visit you, you tried to conceal yourself. Where I wonder? In the pantry? Alternatively, were you skulking beneath the skirts of that dusky wife of yours? Your leaving me was no defiant breaking of the chains - you fled because the Spirit that owns you compelled it. Let us examine your career to date, in the aftermath so to speak. You had a breakdown?'

'I received professional help,' admitted Vicky.

'Bah, only I held the remedy, but you cowered in Sussex, spurning your saviour. Next, let us review your military achievements. Did you appear on the Western Front in shining armour like those angels who materialised above the troops on the eve of Mons? A brilliant invention, incidentally, of my old friend Arthur Machen.'

'It passed like a dream. The mud, the trenches, the only stars those dug into skin by barbed wire. After our experiences, it seemed, incredibly, an anti-climax.'

'You were a slovenly soldier I expect. No doubt such a duffer they sent you home on half pay. This brings us to the cottage provided by your aunt in Steyning, not a fortnight after the Paris Working. Did you fish for trout or take up the mandolin?'

'I published books,' said Vicky.

'Ah yes, the famous Vine Press. Its productions devoured by bishops and statesmen, and acclaimed by critics, stunned by the curious font with the wide W and linked double O, and your own oft-quoted poetry.' Vicky bowed his head. 'And what did become of the sooty charms of that wife of yours, so chimney-swept off her feet by your manly virtues?'

'She ran off with a salesman,' Vickybird croaked.

'You probably paid their fares! And your present situation? You live with someone. Yes! Rather skinny, I expect, a henpecker with a literary bent. Firmly under orders aren't you, Victor, but never starting ones! Then you had that little flush of exposure a couple of years ago. I opened the pages of The Referee and what did I see? My old colleague V.B. Neuburg up to his eyes in the worms and wombs of cocky young pups like the one we met earlier, now presumably fucking Delia at her brothel on the Strand. Where did that little ripple lead? Are you hailed at the Savage? Eulogised in the Criterion? Are you still a Literary Gent?'

'The Referee changed hands. It happened so abruptly.'

'Forcing you once more into the wilderness? What a surprise! Can't you see it all partakes of defeat, material trouble, strife, and every other hallmark of a Flaming One?'

Vicky could stand it no longer. He turned and marched towards the station.

'Were you to walk to the furthermost point of the globe itself you will never escape me,' roared the Beast. 'But Bartzabel you can be free of still.'

'It is you I flee,' cried Vicky. 'You ruined my life!'

'Oh, not that red herring!'

'You squandered my money.'

'On books which revealed the secret of the ages. They will be priceless in a century from now. That was not money wasted.'

'I may not be hailed at the Savage, but then neither are you. Nor do I notice reviews of your books clogging up the columns.'

'The time is not yet ripe. They are seeds. Do you not see?'

'You took my manhood from me. You duped and twisted me. Left me just a shell.'

'How could I steal what was never there? I led you into realms the normal mortal dare not even dream of. You had no bottom! Was that my fault?'

Now alongside the bookshop, Vicky could make out the titles of the ill-assorted second-hand volumes in the window. The Equinox of the Gods was not among them.

'It is typical of you to be so selfish,' the Beast went on. 'Brother Neptunus has arrived, bearing great fortune. By midday tomorrow I could return your money with interest!'

Vicky crossed the narrow street. There was a post box on the corner. It was blue and used solely for airmail. The tube station lay just a few yards on.

'I thought, sentimentally I suppose, we could be friends again. Play chess. Natter on about Enochian and the old days.'

Vicky glared at the metal gates drawn across the station's entrance. Another tart emerged, her business finished, turning wearily out of Cecil Court. Just a couple of old queers having a spat she thought as she passed by.

'Within a year you will be caged in a padded cell and long to smash your brains out in order to evict the visions that torment your dribbling skull!'

No flashes of burning preternatural light illuminated the recesses of the darkened tube; no footsteps scuttled down the frozen escalators fleeing a bombarded city. Nevertheless, Vicky heard again the cold tone of the curse, and because it had never been lifted, he crossed the road.

Crowley greeted him, coming nearer than he had all evening. He stank of Ruthvah.

'Now you must prepare yourself by contemplating the things that pertain to the Spirit you would be released from and who by such attributes is summoned: oak, nettles, pepper, all hot spicy odours.' The Beast tried summoning up such images himself but only managed to evoke an extremely Jupiterean unicorn in a forest of cedars. 'Puff away, Frater Lampada,' he cried. 'Wreath yourself in the clouds of Madim!' Vicky took a deep drag on his Gold Flake, not to summon

Mars, but to expel the panic that was gnawing in his guts.

On the other side of the road Noël Coward's Cavalcade had been revived at the Garrick. Just past this, a billboard exhorted passers-by to "Light a 555." Crowley did not need to reckon up the figures. Such a talisman to the red planet spoke plainly enough - the number was that of Mars! The road curved to the left and alongside now was the National Portrait Gallery. The Beast wondered which of his likenesses would grace the halls if he could not induce Augustus to paint him. John's rather sober sketch of 1906 or Epstein's drawing, which imbued his features with the malevolence of a voodoo doll? If only he had sat for Rodin, whom he had dedicated sonnets to during an assiduous courtship at the outset of the century; or Modigliani, with whom he had sucked hashish from a hookah in that little studio on Montparnasse. However, the Italian had only ever drawn one face, and that had been a child's.

Schemes that were ever more grandiose flooded Crowley's bruised consciousness as they broached the frontiers of Trafalgar Square. Why settle for a portrait screaming for attention in a room full of others? Only a statue would do. But not one like the pious and anodyne memorial to Edith Cavell they had just passed. He gazed up at the column that bore Nelson and saw himself transposed onto that plinth. Rodin was dead unfortunately. Not for the first time Crowley cursed the fact that the time he inhabited was so far ahead of the present. A sculptor in the distant future would have to model him. However, how should he be dressed? In his Chinese robes or his Egyptian ones? No, better this dress coat and Hawes and Curtis waistcoat; top-hatted, a typical Londoner, straining eastwards in salute to the sun, as the Whores of Babylon jostled in their scarlet chariots along the Strand beneath him.

X°
The Bornless Ones

Trafalgar Square was silent. Nothing stirred; not even the pigeons that lined the ledges of the circling buildings in their fast sleep, oblivious to the great event that was about to fall on their domain.

Intent on his magical preparations, Crowley perused the buses drawn up outside the National Gallery, eager for a sign. To a neutral observer the first, a red double decker with Richmond given as its destination, would have presented nothing sinister, but to the trained eye of the Ulema of Thelema the thirty-three on the indicator posed something of a dilemma. Another three and all that night's work would have had to be aborted, for 333 was the number of Choronzon, the baleful demon who had menaced them at Bou Saada. As it was, the sorrow and destruction signified by two threes were bad enough. There was nothing for it but to perform the calling in of the God in the Square; but the calling forth of the Spirit would have to await a more propitious omen.

Accordingly, when flanked on either side by the fountains, Crowley raised his arms and banished the ghosts of Trafalgar, who jostled round the obelisk of their fallen admiral. Then he turned to face the east, where the Portland stone of the recently erected South Africa House gleamed on its bed of granite, and declaimed these words:

'Thee I invoke, the Bornless one.
Thee that didst create the Earth and the Heavens:
Thee that didst create the Night and the Day ... '

His voice went on, soaring and plummeting as it intoned the barbaric names of summoning - 'Blatha, Abeu, Ebeu, Phi'. In themselves the words did not matter - the object was to achieve a state of enflamement in prayer, in which the magician would unite with the God and so control the lesser realms.

'...Come thou forth and follow me:
And make all Spirits subject unto me
So that every Spirit of the Firmament,
And of the Ether: on dry land or in the water:
Of whirling air or of rushing fire:
And every Spell and Scourge of God,
May be obedient unto Me!'

Save for the splashing of the fountains, there was silence when the Beast had finished. The sole occupant of the Square, a policeman who manned the tiny station inside the lamp pillar facing the Strand, had dozed off half an hour before and the Invocation of the Bornless One had not revived him. Unexpectedly, there was a distant clip-clopping and a horse cantered through Admiralty Arch, dragging behind it a hansom cab, the last in London, on its way to prepare for the American tourists and roistering varsity men it would convey round Piccadilly Circus. The Beast seemed satisfied with this omen.

'The horse, like bear and wolf, is sacred to Mars,' he grunted.

The invocation had excited in Vicky a lucid state he remembered from years before. By the time they had crossed to the other side of the Square, however, and were marching down Northumberland Avenue, that and the cocaine were beginning to fade, and he was longing for the comforts of his single bed. Crowley, by contrast, seemed to have shaken off the torpor of the opiates and bubbled with energy as his feet skipped along the pavement.

'Don't you just loathe this mock Tudor?' he said as they passed the Northumberland Hotel with its fake black beams. 'They performed the same abortion on the Wheatsheaf and that hairdresser's in Fleet Street. Why is there such nostalgia for madrigals and the Armada?'

There was horse dung left by milk and dray carts piled at random intervals along the road, which, like the rest of the profuse amounts in London, would be gathered for manure, furnishing industry for some in what were still difficult years. A policeman sauntered out of Great Scotland Yard and registered the oddity of the top-hatted figure and the jittery scarecrow beside him. Appropriately, "An Inspector Calls" was at the Playhouse, and a few yards on Outram, hero of the Indian Mutiny, gazed across the river from his plinth. The statue inspired in Crowley another idea for a memorial. His form as a colossus straddling the Thames, with arms held upwards in the sign of the God Shu supporting the sky, greeting those arriving by water in the west's first City of the Horizon.

The air smelt of river and of the vagrants huddled beneath the arches of Charing Cross Railway Bridge. Turning under one of these, a pair of bloodshot eyes glared up at them from a blanket reeking of meths. Crowley raised his top hat and blessed the startled occupant in a Greek phrase borrowed from the liturgy of the Orthodox Church.

The eastern sky was ringed by light as they emerged onto the Embankment; not in answer to the Beast's prayer, but to the more ancient invocation of the sun.

For Vicky it was a site full of poignancy. It was here his restless steps had taken him, all the way downriver from the Rossetti Studios in Chelsea, after he had told Ione to kill herself. He had stood there at more or less this time, the full August moon poised above the Shot Tower, which still was standing across the river - and out of this turmoil he had written:

"My little wilderness of tangled dreams,
Under the moon-enchanted lonely tower,
 My little land...
Where I pass the morn's first shaded hour -
 My solitude ..."

However, this time he was not alone.

Crowley had turned left, and following, Vicky likewise entered Victoria Embankment Gardens. River mist sealed everything save the circling trees and the vague outlines of Villier's Gate.

'We lack an Altar with Square and Seal of Mars, but here at least is our Triangle, propitiously flourishing with nettles,' announced Crowley.

An area of grass before them, hemmed by two paths that met at its apex and the third on which they stood, formed indeed a perfect triangle. Even more convenient was the circle it ended in, from which all the paths in the Gardens radiated.

'But if the Circle is not properly consecrated,' objected Vicky, 'we shall have no protection.'

This exasperated the Beast. 'Do you not realise that I have attained the ineffable and sublime grade of Ipsissimus and as such am placed beyond all reason and constraint. I no longer need the Pentagon, ruby lamps or any other paraphernalia of magick; nor do I require the haziest notion of Cabbala and Gematria. These are but languages, which like those spoken after Babel, only echo the great vibrations of summoning that can be discovered in the soul. The sky is our true Circle: its dome will guard us.'

Crowley had not entirely dispensed with the ceremonial, however, for steadying the case on his bended thigh, he opened it and removed a single tarot card which he placed on the north-west tip of the Triangle. The card displayed the traditional depiction of the Tower Struck by Lightning of the Golden Dawn, not the Cubist montage of the Beast's own version, still in its genesis. Bending forward, Crowley plunged the steel tip of his cane into the damp earth and traced a scythe-like sign with a curve at one end.

'There, it is done,' he said. "Bartzabel will be summoned by his sigil.'

He straightened and asked the time. It was eighteen minutes to five. 'Capital! Mars is seventeen and a half degrees into Gemini, the exact astrological position of London. The two are perfectly aligned. We could not ask for a more propitious moment for our Working.'

Raising his arms, he turned to the east, where the dome of Saint Paul's shimmered faintly in the burgeoning light, and proceeded to banish the shades of Raleigh and of Leicester. Both had been ferried to execution through the gate palely glimmering to their left, when it had marked the river's boundary, three centuries before thousands of tons of earth had been removed from Haverstock Hill and used to push the waters back. This time the Beast intoned no spell, but wheeled round to face the north-west quadrant of the sky, where Mars, piquantly enough, seemed to hover over Boundary Road.

To raise a Spirit it is necessary to call on a planet's entire chain of command in descending order. This Crowley proceeded to do. 'So come we, O Lord,' he declaimed, 'armed for the holy work of an Evocation of Bartzabel, Spirit of Mars, that is obedient unto the Intelligence Graphiel, chosen from the Seraphim who follow Kamael, the Great Archangel that serves Ye under thy name of Elohim Gibor, a spark from thine intolerable flame!'

Bands of uneven light straddled the lawn, which in the twilight and swirling mist could easily have tricked the eye into making out a form. However, with the slightest shake of his head, Crowley launched into a series of imprecations, which Vicky, with the glee of a man eating after a long fast, joined him in, offering with the Beast to be burnt and consumed by the Red Eye of Mars should the Spirit not be summoned. Again, there was nothing. But then the random mist seemed to coalesce into a pillar of smoke at the centre of the Triangle, which dissolving, revealed a dishevelled woman wearing a veil adorned with wilted roses and a dress that hung down like a tattered bridal gown.

'What can you make out?' shrieked Crowley, who suffered the great misfortune for a magician, akin to that of deafness for a composer, of being incapable of apprehending visions. It was because of this he needed more sensitive types, such as Neuburg or Loveday, to scry for him.

'It is Delia,' said Vickybird. 'She must have lost Dylan and followed us here.'

'It is no such thing,' snapped Crowley. 'Have you forgotten how Choronzon assumed the shape of a woman in order to undo us? Address whatever it is and demand to know when the Kingdom of the Aeon will be established.'

'Not in the year of the three kings,' - it was the Spectre's voice gliding monotously out until it was lost amidst the branches of the trees - 'nor before the living dig trenches for the dead and are themselves killed and toppled into them. Then men will wash their faces with another's and read Holderlin beneath lamps whose shades are made of skin.'

Vicky repeated what he had heard.

'Three kings?' Crowley seemed puzzled. Then the import of the words struck him. 'Of course, the Star Sapphire, that great talisman of the realm, fell from the hearse of George the Fifth; and Cheiro, blast him for the charlatan he never was, predicted back in twenty-five that Edward would lose the throne because of a woman. We shall indeed have three kings this year. However, these novel forms of soap and lighting make no sense. Demand what they might be.'

'Death will become a document tedious for some: ninety-three scrawled on a cattle truck rattling past a field of skulls; two-four-nine screaming in a burning barn; the stench of gas asphyxiating five-four-one; torture resurrected, bombardment by plane and rocket trebling the score.'

'Ninety-three is the number of the Thelemic current,' said Crowley, 'five-four-one of Israel, but the rest of her apocalyptic drivel leads nowhere. Exact from her when the Warrior Lord of the Forties will appear.'

'He already struts among you. He counts his term a Thousand but will be given only Twelve.'

'Then the epoch of the Beast will be unleashed?' cried Crowley, thrilling himself.

'Of Beasts, certainly,' came the reply.

'Conjunct with the Aeon of Horus?'

'Of no God you could name, though you know so many. But desist from your prying, for Dylan has forsaken me and I am weary and find no succour from you, not even a thumbnail of cocaine.'

Folds of mist unpicked the figure and momentarily obscured the lawn. A bird began singing on a distant branch but thought better of it. The folds parted once more and another form stood there. Vicky found he was gazing on a face he had long imagined devoured by worms - the lovely features of Ione.

'Victor,' she murmured. 'I am so cold. Come to me here and warm me.'

Conveyed by her voice was the vulnerability that had made him long to nurture and shield her. His feet shuffled forwards till the tips of his shoes almost brushed the perimeter of the Triangle. He only had to reach out to stroke the tresses of waist-length hair and trace the whiteness of her cheek, highlighted by the pale blue powder she employed for just such a purpose. One step, and she would murmur her forgiveness. Crowley's talons gripped his arm.

'Do not step into the Triangle be it the Lord of Hosts himself who calls you!'

'I always hated those signs that said don't tread on the grass. Besides, it is Ione.'

'That siren! That snake in the grass plying her wiles to bind you in tresses that will hoop you like rings of steel! Be gone, Blood-Sucker!'

'It is he not I who is the Vampire,' countered the apparition in a flat, carefully modulated voice that was oddly like the Spectre's. 'Oh Victor, why do you still consort with him after all the wrong he did us?'

'She slanders me I expect. Are you going to founder on her rocks again? She is not Ione at all, but a wraith jealous of our substance.'

The apparition made no answer but raised her pale arms to the top of the same white tunic she had worn when she had been Luna in the Rites, and tugged the straps down so the garment fell to the ground. A familiar body, with tiny breasts that blushed at the nipples and a triangle of down, fanned in Vicky the impulse to hurl himself forward, a desire impeded by the Beast who had moved round and clenched him from behind.

'In the name of Elohim Gibor,' he cried, 'I banish you to depart, failed and spiteful Spirit, and return to whence you came to torment yourself with your lack of substance. By Kamael the great Angel and by the Intelligence Graphiel that rules you, I conjure your dispatch to the realm of shadows that is your rightful domain.'

The mist became a whirlpool swirling round the Triangle then dispersed taking the apparition with it. A full minute passed as they stood there with Vicky locked in Crowley's trembling arms, not in the posture of love as formerly, but in that of fear.

At last the Scryer spoke, his voice shaking: 'This has gone too far.'

'Too far to stop,' countered Crowley, slowly relaxing his grip. 'Are you going to run away again? I offered you release and that deliverance is but minutes hence if you do not flinch!' His voice becoming sonorous he cried: 'I do conjure thee, O thou Spirit Bartzabel, by all the most glorious and efficacious names of the Most Great Incomprehensible Lord of Hosts, that thou comest quickly and without delay from the sphere of Mars to make rational answers unto my questions.'

Accompanied by the gestures of arms now free of Vicky, he continued to exhort the Spirit, by a whole pantheon of names and admonitions, to appear before them. First light nestled on the branches of the elms, transposing silver on the grey. Blue, in patches, was appearing in the sky. From the direction of the Savoy, a horn blared - a muezzin announcing daybreak for the traffic. The Triangle remained empty.

'Perhaps only a sexual rite will do,' muttered Crowley pacing the Circle. Seeing Vicky's consternation, he quickly added, 'Have no fear! Does a wrinkled beast lust after a goat? Curse that woman! She has botched this Working almost as she did the Rites. Oh that fickle and mendacious tribe that forever blights the Will of Man.'

'Having come so far, did you think I would not visit you?' demanded a voice coming from the Triangle.

It was a face familiar from a thousand newsreels, caricatured that very year by Chaplin in "The Great Dictator". However, in truth the sneering visage was much older, belonging as it did to the Bartzabel of the North, whom the German tribes called Wotan. Decked in a long red cloak flecked with black that resembled a volcano in eruption, the Flaming One towered over them, so tangible that Vicky recalled the hallucinations of mescal but was loath to calibrate such substance by a drug.

'You should be apparent to he you possess, not I who has no truck with you.' protested Crowley. He was severely flustered. Though long used to letting others endure unhinging visions, he was not accustomed to seeing them himself.

'Then choose what to see, you to whom all is arbitrary, and have me vanish. After you can unmake the moon and have the stars disperse.' The eyes were like red coals in the white face. There was a notable warmth, but the voice was icy. 'I am here obedient not to your summons but to my Will. Now is my time to walk abroad: the age demands it.'

'You are confined within the Triangle I have designated, summoned here by the conjurations I have made. I compel you to obey me, Bartzabel, or like Solomon I will bind you in a box of brass that shall not be broken even at the End of Time.'

'Do pearls adorn the necks of goats? Do the Elohim fill a latrine with roses? I tell you, Conjuror, I am here of my own volition and by its edict only shall I depart.'

'Mighty and appareled though you seem the merest spell could unmake you.'

'Then mouth it and watch me vanish.'

'Not till you have fulfilled the purpose of this calling, which is to depart utterly from the man Victor Neuburg.'

'Do you think I need such a paltry life as his to make my spells? My work is plentiful; everywhere men marshal to my cause.'

'Vain Spirit singing your own praises like a witless fool. You who reigned in Edom before a King ruled over Israel and were usurped by your own folly.'

The being frowned: 'Sad Kings we were, broken and desolate. Yet we were raised to the dignity of the spheres.'

'Then by the unpronounceable name of the Lord of Hosts, which if spoken spells the end of all things, I command you to return there. By this sign also shall I make you flee.'

Crowley's hand sliced through the air, his fingers seemingly trailing fire that left the imprint of a six-sided figure - the Hexagram of Earth that is used to banish planets.

The head of the figure disappeared into clouds of smoke. These billowed from what was now a small volcano, whose cone jutted upwards from the lawn. At the same moment, a large bird swooped between the magicians, so close that Vicky felt the wind of its wings.

The falcon hurtled on towards the gate, flew between the columns of lichen-covered stone and vanished. With a mescal-like intensity, whirling bands of scarlet and emerald appeared in its place, before which rose a platform of stone connecting the two sides of the arch. A form stepped onto this eminence, a lion's tail dragging after the scarlet sandals. Crowley gasped, and tugging Vicky with him, crumpled to his knees.

'I am looking for the Plagiarist.'

The words crashed like a wave through the gate having no tangible source in the maelstrom within, for the beak of the newcomer remained clenched shut.

Awe, never a frequent visitor, had vanished from Crowley's face, replaced by a more typical petulance. He raised his head and so did Vicky. Their eyes met the piercing gaze of a giant whose head was that of a falcon, tawny and black, and body entirely scarlet. On his head was a crown and in his right hand an emerald wand. Everything about him was lively, as though at any moment he would burst into flame.

'You stood behind me in that room in Cairo,' remonstrated Crowley. 'Every word of the Book of the Law you dictated.'

'That was not my voice,' the answer rolled over them like a tidal wave. 'Aiwass was the messenger of Set, prince of destruction, brother and murderer of Osiris, called in your time Satan. You were duped by the devil! Useless bungler, how tiresome you have become to the Gods who laugh mirthlessly at your vanity. Why do you not go back to Plymouth and the Brethren you never left, Eater of Shit?'

'I see now,' said Crowley slowly rising, 'that you are but one more illusion, aping the great master whose harbinger I am in order to torment me.'

Like a blast from a furnace, a wave of heat forced them back.

'I am not a salamander and must licence you to depart, Spirit!'

'I am no Spirit; I am the Lord of the Horizon, the Winged Disc of the Sun! How should I address you - Ipsissimus? As if you could partake of one spark of the unbearable light that dazzles Kether. Will you not join me in the Square as you did Choronzon, Serpent of Daath, so I can peck out your eyes with my beak and tear you limb from limb with my talons?'

'If I thought for one moment you were truly Horus, the Crowned and Conquering child, I would rush to greet you. But you will not entice me, thing of straw that ignites when the burning eye of Mars is unlidded, which I now bid open and consume you utterly.'

An orgy of heat fanned from the arch, driving them out of the Circle. Crowley was forced back along the path and Vicky onto the triangle of grass, now free of the smoke that veiled the periphery of trees, but not the river, which appeared, glimmering with mooring lights from piers and barges, through a parting in the branches.

'Do you suppose, creature of slime wading in a swamp, that the marsh-lights you have seen were real or you will be permitted to pass through these firmaments and enter into the Kingdom of Light? Do you not realise you are but a maggot wriggling in the slime deposited by mounds of waste?'

'Are you so ignorant,' Crowley shouted hoarsely back, 'that you do not understand that you and the great ones of the emanation of light are all made out of the same matter, paste and substance as myself? However, you, in purifying yourselves, have not been in affliction, whereas I, who am indeed the debris of the stars, suffer and am forlorn through being poured into a body of this world. Know that when by my sufferings I have purged myself, I will go on high to the

Kingdom of Light and will be revered because I am the refuse of the dross and have become purer than you all.'

A crackle came from the Square, but of scorn not flame.

'Preposterous man, do you suppose to trounce me with such Gnostic sophistries? The shades of Agrippa and Paracelsus vomit on the blasphemies of your tedious books. Blake wipes his arse with your misprints. Logos of the Aeon? You are its clown!'

'No, I am the Columbus of the soul, the great discoverer. The Gods love my blasphemies because through them their existence is affirmed.'

'Oh must I hear again the futile delusions of the Templars and Cathars? Like them you are nothing but a bugger!'

The God raised his right arm and pointed the wand across the river. Out of the cloudless sky, a bolt of lightning flashed down and struck the top of the Shot Tower. Around it appeared wavering beams of light: searchlights probing an ashen sky. From the east came a rumbling, then wave upon wave of planes, the fighters clustered round the bombers like drones. These were the emissaries of the Blitzkrieg so long feared, which would reduce London to rubble in a week and leave a race of troglodytes abject in the tubes; this, the terrible war whose prospect made Baldwin and Halifax so craven before Hitler.

Crowley seemed exhilarated by the spectacle. It was a prophecy of the Book of Law fulfilled. 'Choose ye an island,' he warbled. 'Fortify it! Dung it about with enginery of war!'

There were explosions from the docks and smoke puffed over hidden wharves, more flashes, until the red glare of the blazing wax in the warehouses of St Katherine's Dock lit the sky. The wax streamed across the quays and sluiced into the docks, where it formed a hard sheet across the water. The flames rose two hundred feet, reddening the Thames into a limb of Horus.

A siren wailed from the railway station and as it faded, there came a droning from across the river. This was quickly followed by the crash of glass and the rumble of buildings caved in by the explosions, then the unlikeliest sound of all - the frantic whinnying of shire horses as they galloped out of the bombed brewery beside the Shot Tower. There was a drone from overhead.

Looking up, Vicky saw a Zeppelin nosing through the barrage balloons. An explosion came from the road. The blast flung Crowley onto concrete and Vicky onto grass. The dirigible had also been hit. It burst into flame and fell slowly at first, casting another sheen on a river already dazed by reflections. Soon, crushed beneath a twisted mass of steel, its gondolas settled on the water and compelled the drowning of any of the aircrew not already burnt alive. There was the sound of ragged cheering, snuffed out as rapidly as it had begun; and then that of ack-ack guns chattering like the teeth of a music-hall skull. A wall of flame encircled the Gardens, which dissembled in places to reveal the brief impediment of the river and the whole of Southwark on fire.

XI°
The Oracle of Dawn

A short way from the Embankment Gardens, the guests of the Savoy remained indifferent to the sorcerers' predicament. No landmine had fallen, rocking the hotel and shattering every window facing the river, or bomb struck the parapet over the entrance in the Strand - that all lay five years in the future. Instead, autonomous as an ocean liner, the hotel sailed serenely through the night, pampering its guests with food, fine wines, and laundry that was available even when not required, as the man in the silk dressing gown on the eighth floor had just discovered.

'This really is a most extraordinary time...!' he began, but then shut up. The corpulent intruder on the threshold, in his white laundryman's coat buttoned to the throat, did not carry the change of towels that had been promised from the other side of the door; furthermore, he was repeating a phrase his listener recognised as a sure token of the Beast: the Oracle of Dawn, indeed, was Brilliance. How typical of the Master to add an unexpected touch, for the grinning speaker was a Chinaman.

Brother Neptunus, who appeared on the hotel register under his real name of Karl Hammer, hurried the man into the private suite and locked the door behind them. Crossing the main corridor with its deep crimson carpet and lofty ceiling, they came to an immense bedroom on one side and an equally vast lounge on the other. Hammer gestured towards the latter. It was a zone of brocaded upholstery and an abundance of lamps, cushions and occasional tables. Everything is as soft as this nervous man, thought Loke.

Except for the area around the desk, lit up by a banker's lamp, the room was pitched in shadow. The curtains were still undrawn, but the sheen that filtered in from the river was the glow of lampposts and mooring lights, not the glare of searchlights and explosions. Hammer's English was so impeccable as he offered his visitor a drink from the bottle of whisky on the sideboard it was obvious he was foreign. Loke refused. It was bad luck to accept hospitality from a victim.

A grey Homburg hung from the back of the chair at the desk. The German padded over to it, the light picking out the features of a once handsome face becoming ordinary beneath thinning fair hair. Crowley had nicknamed this scion of a family of industrialists, who had swelled his coffers since converting to Thelema in the early Thirties, "The Rich Man of the Ruhr". Hammer lifted the hat by its rim, and with his other hand, took a letter opener from the desk, speaking rapidly as he did so in a refined, weaselly voice: 'You are from the Beast?'

Loke agreed that he was.

'Canaris sent me because the Nazis are on the point of proscribing all magical societies in Germany. The Black Brothers do not like the competition. They will round up everyone in the O.T.O. and bundle them off to concentration camps. I have to establish myself in

England. As a Lord, the Beast must be able to furnish me with connections.'

'You need something?' Loke had only half-understood the words but was quite familiar with the tone.

'Do you not realise who you're dealing with?' Anger made Hammer shrill. 'He is the greatest figure of our time - more than Hitler: more even than Sun Yat-Sen.'

This came as something of a revelation. Loke considered Crowley to be a fat man who liked opium and whores.

'Still, there might be one thing,' the German went on as he tore at the hat's lining with the letter opener's blade. A rip and it gave way. Transferring the opener to his other hand, he withdrew a package wrapped in brown paper.

Loke had guessed what he was after. 'You want see picture?' He delved into the pocket of his coat and removed a wallet, from which he produced a photograph, which he passed to Hammer. A girl in a skimpy corset pouted up at him. Wondering how far she would go - the routine Tenth? The profane Eleventh? – Hammer's eyes strayed from the picture to the three-signal bell-tablet: Maid, Valet, Waiter. He would press the last, deciding on Bollinger '23, Oysters and two haddock Côte d'Azur. Absorbed in designing this love feast, he was unaware of Loke moving up behind and the noiseless way the knife was produced. The Chinaman flicked the switch, so the blade sprung out in ironic homage to the erection the German would now never entertain, and plunged the knife into the fleshy part at the back of the neck - Hammer's spinal column severed with a snap.

It was a death without histrionics. The very opulence of the room colluded with its perpetrator. The dense walls and soundproofed casements baffled the cry and ensuing death rattle; the pile carpet soaked up the blood; the fresh-washed air, streaming from the air-conditioning, dispersed the smell.

Loke bent down, extracted the package from Hammer's still trembling fingers, then crossed to the window. After wiping his weapon on the curtain, he used the blade to tear through the paper.

There was the Abwehr's fee as arranged - a neat bundle of thousand Reichmark notes. There was the diamond. He cradled it in his palm. Nearly as big as a plover's egg, the subdued light transformed its blue facets into a prism. Inserting the money in his wallet and jewel in the pocket of his coat, he unlocked the door and went out into the hall.

The corridor evoked a ship. It lacked only portholes. Loke resolved to return to China in robes as silken as the wallpaper he padded past. A man in a brown trilby with a turned down rim was approaching with a mince like that of the male prostitutes the Chinaman had often seen in Soho Square.

Captain King was thinking of the scene of abjection in the suite he had just left. It made him wonder if the rumours were true and the King would soon be playing baby to Wallis's nanny. However, his was a degradation just as profound. He had a weakness for mechanics and barrow boys. This bent had already compelled his first wife to kill herself and was turning the second into a wraith. Realising he was observed; he quickly adopted a stiff martial stride. Loke bowed his head. There was something about the stranger now that conjured images of passport offices.

Sounds were coming from the suite ahead. Loke darted a look at the face passing him - a frown depressed it. Hurrying on, the Chinaman came adjacent to the door. A rasping American voice was listing the faults of the "mouse" she was with. They seemed endless.

He had kept the Japanese Ambassador waiting half an hour; he had not had the guts to abolish the thirty-pound bonus paid annually to palace staff for livery; he was not standing up enough to Baldwin.

Loke's hand dived into his coat pocket and clutched the jewel. Chang was right. It was too good for the American bitch who had ensnared the King. The sacrifice of Hammer had been more than merited, as would that of the Beast and his scrawny colleague.

'I'm most abysmally sorry,' Loke heard the King blub. 'I don't get the low-down on anything about life, except it's foul and cruel and difficult. I'm so glum and bewildered by it all.'

'Stop your snivelling, David,' she said in her hard voice, 'and take me to the river.'

*

Ignorant of their new peril, Crowley had scrambled to his feet and was walking slowly back along the path, seemingly unperturbed by the inferno Horus had unleashed. With a Churchillian frown he lifted his hand and formed with the digit and middle finger a V - not that of Victory, but of Khem, or ancient Egypt.

'You are privileged to witness the destruction of the world by fire,' he growled.

'It is the coming war we glimpse,' gasped Vicky.

'You never get it, do you? What you are seeing occurred on March the twentieth, 1904.'

'But we live and breathe three decades after.'

Yet, even as he spoke, Vicky noted the conflagration did seem to be total. Not just the south of the river, but York buildings and the eighteenth century Adams houses backing on to the Embankment Gardens, all partook of the blaze.

'Do you really live and breathe?' hissed Crowley. 'Besides, what I have told is according to the initiated doctrine. In the instant of the Book of the Law's transmission the world expired!'

He hurled himself forward, and with a deft sideward stroke plunged his cane through the sigil, cutting the magical current. There was a whistling, the wailing of a bird, and suddenly two middle-aged English gentlemen, who had entertained some eccentric notions, were standing in the tranquillity of the Embankment Gardens on a roseate dawn in early June.

Crowley, who seemed remarkably unflustered by their ordeal, spoke first: 'I had forgotten how spectacular things get when you're around. A most successful Working I should say.'

'But Horus disowned you,' objected Vicky. 'He heaped derision on your system.'

'That wasn't Horus,' snapped Crowley as though addressing a child, 'that was a piece of puff like those dreamed up by Weary Willie Yeats. Blake fashioned an intricate casket and heaped it with pearls: that dishevelled Irish demonologist made a toilet bowl and filled it full of shit. I'm surprised we didn't glimpse a druid.'

'But what we saw was real,' insisted Vicky.

'I grant you it was impressive,' said Crowley, taking Vicky by the arm and leading him affably up the path. 'Apart from a couple of goblins in the Alps, and an evocation of Buer I performed in the early days, which was rewarded with a helmet suggestive of Athena, part of a tunic and some very solid footwear, the veil has trembled little in my case. But the trappings of that apparition were no more the property of a demon than what we saw tonight partook of Horus.'

A few feet ahead, the path dissolved into pavement. Railings stretched down both sides of the Embankment, hemming in the bushes and trees whose leaves unfurled above.

Crowley paused. 'I do not think I have had a run in like that since I stayed with that Russian fellow in Fontainebleau, what all of a decade ago. Gurdjieff was excessively polite until it was time to leave. "You been guest?" ' - No mean actor, the Beast mimicked the Russian accent rather well - 'I could hardly deny it: for the entire weekend I had been fattened on duck and steeped in pepper vodka. Then having, I suppose, made the point that his hospitality was at an end, the dear fellow launched into a blistering attack, startlingly similar to that which I have so recently endured. However, I am forgetting you, Victor. How does it feel to be released?'

'It is as though for twenty years I have been locked with a maniac in a stuffy room and suddenly am free! I feel like letting rip with a hey-nonny-non!'

Crowley peered at him quizzically. 'Though Mars won't get you his Herb Dangerous tobacco probably will. Your deliverance is temporary; but for what there is of it you have the good Master Therion to be grateful to.'

'It is he I must thank for the problem in the first place!'

Crowley broke into passable cockney. 'I was just moonin' abaht mindin' me own business when along comes this wicked geezer who dropped me in it. Must I forever put up with the whingeing of my so-called victims? But for me your life would have been unspeakably mundane! What were your good, generous aunts intent on you taking up? The family business!' He spat out the words as though they were the most hideous he had ever uttered. 'You could have been an importer of cane and rattan; while I, of course, should still be in Leamington brewing beer.'

'We went too far. We saw further than is permitted.'

'You have witnessed things the rest of the century scarcely dreams of, Victor! And don't throw Nietzsche at me. Even when you stop trilling and talk about something real, you cannot be original! You have had firsthand experience of Pan and Mars, as well as the Greatest Living Englishman, for I am sure the Gods will jostle to have me on the pantheon, yet you are skewered by remorse for that flea-bitten trollop Ione. What, incidentally, led you to understand I did not have her? Was she so special?'

A ragged smile breached the corners of Vicky's lips. The truth was something he would not disclose to the Beast, just as he had never revealed it to anyone. If any secret died with him, it would be that Ione's smallness meant she could never know a man in the normal sense. Vicky had therefore possessed her as he had the Beast - his seed had fallen into darkness. It was this, he believed, that had killed her: the knowledge she could never be a woman. Unbidden an image arose of her prone before him, compared to Crowley, a lily to a thorn.

'Bah!' exclaimed the Beast, disgruntled by this lack of enlightenment. 'It will be Rome next for you, my boy. Any wizened bugger of a priest will absolve you. You may even give up smoking,'

'I've never been one to recant,' objected Vickybird with spirit. 'I believed in our experiment, but the cost!'

'Harping on about money again?'

'I meant to the spirit.'

'Finally formed one, have you?' the Beast was all contempt.

They had emerged from the Gardens, and before them, on the opposite side of the road, a curious scene was unfolding. A van bearing the words "London Films" on its side was parked about twenty yards down from the first of the sphinxes, which flanked Cleopatra's Needle. A man in a brown trilby was in the passenger seat reading a newspaper. On the pavement alongside a team of technicians were mounting lights, while a short tubby individual, a few feet from them, was barking instructions to two cameramen. Loitering against the wall of the Embankment was a crowd of actors dressed in Egyptian costumes.

'Good, they are here!' said Crowley, startling Vicky who found such a reception committee the oddest so far of all the night's proceedings.

A light switched on, swivelled on its mountings, and momentarily dazzled them. Was it this he had seen in the Gardens, the ultimate marsh-light engineering at a crucial juncture the rest of an illusion? He cursed the destiny that led him always to this doubt.

'Look, A.C, I know there's more to this than meets the eye of a P.I.B. like me. Everything you do seems to be part of a plan, but I just don't get it.'

The Beast sighed. 'Magical thinking does have its drawbacks. Even deciding what to wear for dinner becomes a maze.'

'Now you won't find me singing "Tipperary". I am an Internationalist at heart. But I will have no truck with intrigue with a foreign power!'

'How dare you, Sir!'

'You were accused of treason in the Great War!'

'It was no such thing. It is true in America I proposed Britain be made a German colony and burnt my British passport on the steps of the Statue of Liberty. As editor of Fatherland, I even printed a list of targets for Count Zeppelin, which included the address of my horrible

Aunt Ada in Addiscombe. However, I was acting a part. My brief was to make German propaganda ludicrous, and anyone who read my glorification of the Kaiser, would have to agree I succeeded admirably. I should have received the V.C. for my efforts!'

The Beast sounded sincere, but you could never really tell.

'Why didn't this come out?' demanded Vicky.

'The chiefs of British and American Naval Intelligence were privy to exactly what I was doing, but of course they wouldn't admit it. If I really was a traitor, how was it when I returned to England in 1919 I was not hanged upon the spot? I suppose it was fortunate Count Zeppelin ignored my advice, for I took up residence at my detested aunt's, and received nothing worse than a trouncing in John Bull.'

'What about your "friends in Berlin"?'

'Victor, do you really know nothing of the smokescreens and subterfuge that attend matters of high state? I will have you know, almost single-handedly, I am on the point of saving the King from a ruinous marriage with a clapped-out geisha in league with our enemies. Undoubtedly, I will be showered with gifts by a grateful nation.'

Like a guttering wick flaring up for one last time, the prospect seemed to fill Crowley with enthusiasm. He ringed his arm through Vicky's. 'On the proceeds I've been thinking of starting up the Abbey again. Place in the country with farm attached. Make our young disciples work for their supper, eh! Of course, I do not want to be too closely identified with the project. I would stay in the background, a sort of grey eminence, if you like. Now I do not know why I am proposing this after your base insinuation, but I need someone like you out front. There would be an Inner Order and an Outer one. You can head the latter. We will call you Brother He Who Dropped the Torch and Picked it up Again. I wonder what that would be in Latin.'

For a moment, Vicky felt the pull of the idea. He was a man without occupation, frittering away his time on sterile projects. Crowley's scheme would make him a "somebody" again. He could bask in the attention of the unbalanced young, who would no doubt flock to the Abbey; glow once more with the sort of prestige he had enjoyed at the Sanctuary, a haven of long-haired artists not far from Steyning he had frequented in the Twenties. However, when he looked at the portly gentleman shambling along beside him, he realised this was no great poet nor mystic, no god nor demon, but a man as perplexed as anyone else by what he should be doing. As the Christian twilight had fallen they had proclaimed a New Age - Orage had even named his magazine after it. But would that age really find its motto to be a selfish phrase pinched from Rabelais and its creed a pantheon of vanished gods, no matter how stirring their names? Did it really need an avatar obsessed by drugs, orgasms and the texture of a woman's shit? With release from Bartzabel had come unexpected deliverance from the Beast.

'Well, no matter.' Crowley sounded weary and asked the time.

The question provided a welcome opportunity for Vicky to free his arm. Earth from his fall in the Gardens smeared his Omega. He rubbed it off, careless of the soil transferring to his fingers. 'Seventeen minutes past six,' he said.

'In five minutes it will begin.'

'Whatever else could possibly occur?' objected Vicky.

'Well, for one thing we might run into an old friend,' Crowley chuckled, waving his cane at the bench they were approaching. Sprawled upon it, the check suit crumpled, the shoes more stained than those of the tramp they had passed under the arches, was Dylan fast asleep and snoring heavily. 'But is he the same man we met in the Gargoyle? I somehow doubt it.'

Crowley went up to the sleeping poet and prodded him in the stomach. Dylan came to with a start.

'What's this?' he muttered blearily. 'A couple of poetry inspectors come to read my metre?'

'Indeed, Sir, we are emissaries of much weightier import,' answered the Beast. 'I should really find a few more representatives of the races, but I suppose a Jew and Taffy will have to do.'

Swansea's Villon blinked and unsteadily hauled himself upright, using the brass armrests to help him. In deference to the Egyptian theme of the area, they were inscribed with hieroglyphs.

'I'm really swilling the rancid bitters of Life No.13. If you don't mind, I'd rather stay put till the dervish stops whirling.'

Crowley was stern: 'I'm offering you a window on eternity in the presence of the deathless Gods. What poet would not crave that?'

'Right now I'd prefer a two up, two down in Rookery Nook with a nice missus making tea and sarnies.'

'Threw you out, did she?'

Dylan fuzzily considered this: 'I was as sick as a ventriloquist and stained her dressing table a pleasing yellow.'

'Was this before or after the sacrifice?'

Dylan blinked and ran one hand through the tousled mop of his hair. He did not seem to know.

'Delia is like Portsmouth: open to all comers at any hour!' There was a note of menace in Crowley's voice.

Dylan tried to recall a night whose incidents floated like scum on turbulent waters. He remembered the complications of releasing the Spectre from her satin gown. Her flesh had been pasty and unhealthy looking; an effect accentuated by the blackness of the gloves she had not bothered to remove. Rose petals from her veil had strewn the bed when he had finished. His head was pounding. Was there really a price to pay?

'No hocus?' he demanded.

'My magick is as authentic as your verse.'

Dylan hoisted himself to his feet, noticing the film crew as he did so.

'I shall want my usual fee.'

Crowley stepped out into the deserted road and began crossing towards the foot of Cleopatra's Needle. Vicky, however, stood rooted to the curb. The object before them, cheerfully misattributed by Londoners to the Egyptian Queen, had been raised by an altogether different pharaoh he remembered.

'The Place of Dawn is the obelisk of Thothmes,' he murmured, repeating Crowley's mantra.

'Bit florid, don't you think? Some might say wilfully obscure,' said Dylan, who was using his old editor as a crutch. This was a definite case of the pot calling the kettle. 'The pubs will be opening in Fleet Street in about ten minutes,' he hissed. 'Why don't we leave Thelma to her pocus, hop in a taxi and have a gargle? You look like you need one, Vickybird.'

Crowley was beckoning impatiently for them to cross. Like a marionette, Vickybird jerked his bandy legs forward taking Dylan with him. They negotiated the tramlines, mounting first the pavement, then the steps that led onto the platform. Beside them was the pedestal, cemented into which were Bradshaw's Railway Guide, submarine cables, the photographs of a dozen pretty Englishwomen, and other tributes of a more gung-ho civilisation.

High tide had sluiced the topmost of the river stairs, and along the wall, the mottled stone lions were lapping up the dank green Thames. However, across the river, where no meddlesome engineer had erected an embankment, the water shrugged at mud banks strewn with planks and ripped-up tyres, on which seagulls perched. Then, like fireflies seeking mates amongst the lights of the film crew, the rays of the risen sun came flooding through the greyness. Light nuzzled the roofs of Lambeth, gilded Waterloo Bridge, streaked across the dome of Saint Paul's and the bend in the river, simultaneously glinting on one, shimmering on the other. Then it waxed the obelisk, glancing from the brass snakes and scarabs coiled at its base.

Crowley stepped forward, stretched out his arms, and facing eastwards cried, 'Hail unto thee who art Ra in Thy rising, even unto Thee who art Ra in Thy strength; who travellest over the Heavens in Thy bark at the uprising of the Sun. Hail unto Thee from the Abodes of Dawn.'

The hands of the clock on the Shell-Mex building had just passed six twenty. Vicky noticed the actors gazing up at them, not with reverence but envy, as though the Beast's performance had capped the ones they were about to give. Even the man on the passenger seat of the van had lowered his newspaper. Despite such a reception, however, no camera was trained upon Crowley who proceeded to open the case, remove a book and flourish it before him, oblivious both to the clanging of a tram emerging from the arches and the slow progress of a silver Daimler that had come out of Savoy Place and pulled up a hundred yards away. There was a sandy haired man and woman with the face of a white doll within.

'Do what thou wilt shall be the whole of the Law,' cried Crowley. 'I, Ankh-f-n-Khonsu, the Priest of the Princes, present the representatives of the races with The Book of the Law. It is a charter of universal freedom for every man and woman in the world. Love is the law, love under will.'

The tram pulled away, leaving an obese man with a receding hairline and flat features. He hesitated as he took in the scene. Then crossing the road he grinned, not at them, not at the actors, but because grinning was his face's natural attitude.

Vicky grinned back, then broke into a peel of raucous laughter so loud it astonished the pigeons who reeled indignantly from their perches on the brass dolphins at the base of the lampposts, their shadows speckling the Embankment like falling leaves. Vickybird was laughing because he had assumed the crew was there to film the climax of the Beast's career and realised now how absurd that was. It was like believing Brilliant Chang's nephew was another "representative of the races" come to mill in homage around the Logos of the Aeon. This reflection excited another screech.

'Victor!' Crowley grasped his arm and pinched it until it hurt.

The actor had shifted his gaze and was examining the newcomer with extraordinary intensity. The Chinaman turned, met this stare, and understanding it, broke into a run that was surprisingly fleet given his girth, eastwards, towards the Daimler. Stepping completely out of character, the actor pulled a Webley out of his scarabed belt, aimed and fired. Loke stumbled and almost fell. A stain had appeared on the left sleeve of his coat, not lurid as in films, but dull and disappointing, as though someone had slung a pat of mud at him.

Now it was the turn of the gulls on the other side of the river to flutter squawking from their hoards. The Chinaman's right hand dived into his pocket and removed an object. In the same split second another shot was fired. This time no modest and implausible stain appeared, but the back of Loke's head burst open and his brains spilled out. The force of the blast spun him round. Flung from his hand, the jewel traced a narrow arc and plunged into the river.

The Daimler's engines roared into life. It swerved across to the other side of the Embankment and thundered off in the direction of Somerset House. Crowley relaxed his grip, his face ashen, the bloodless lips that had quivered with so many barbaric names, now utterly at a loss for words.

The actor loped past them and crouched down next to Loke. He rifled through his pockets, found the flick-knife and a wallet but nothing more, then turned and shrugged in the direction of the van. A door slammed angrily, but the man in the brown trilby sashayed towards them as though all this was but a brief diversion on his morning stroll.

Leaving Dylan, busily retching up the last contents of his guts, Vicky thudded down the steps and confronted the newcomer beside the shrapnel-marked pedestal of the right-hand Sphinx. The shadow of an overhanging elm darkened an object on the paving stone between them. Captain King gazed at the river, the sunlight soaping his face into a shiny oval.

'The Blue Sapphire of Mysore, cherished by the Moguls,' he sighed. 'The Abwehr stole it in India and brought it through Turkey just for this. Now we must find another way to scotch Wallis.'

The other secrets they shared, those of a more esoteric ilk, must sanction such disclosures, thought Vicky. Otherwise, he was at a loss to explain them.

There was a crunch from the top of the stairs. Crowley stood above them; his gaze not blank and pitiless but oddly futile. 'In your different ways you have all betrayed me,' he cried. 'Yet witness! I have stayed true to my Magical Oath. I swore not to retain one material possession and never to admit of love. This I promised to the Work, and behold am I not now stripped of everything? The gem lies in the river, and you, my friends, rebuke me. Yet I shall endure!'

There was the blast of a foghorn as a barge emerged from beneath the Railway Bridge. Vicky gazed at the Shot Tower. There was hardly a cloud, no bolt or fork of lightning.

Captain King moved closer and said in a low voice. 'My first wife and I were drawn into A.C.'s circle shortly before her suicide. Some might say his influence tipped the scales, but he did not kill her. There were other things…' Remembering the terrible day she had stumbled on him with the young mechanic, he bowed his head and so sighted the dead bird on the pavement. Bending down he scooped it up. 'How curious!' he exclaimed in the avuncular tone that in the Fifties would endear him to a generation of children, when under his real name of Maxwell Knight, he became a celebrated broadcaster on natural life. 'A falcon killed it. Look at the marks left where the toothed edge of the predator's bill snapped the neck. That's something I've never seen in London.'

On a branch above Vicky, a chaffinch bursts into song. Crowley broods upon the river and his lost fortune. Captain King contemplates the broken bird. In such stillness, Thoth assumes his licence to depart.

The End

Afterword

Known to him or not a writer invokes, and being possessed, is permitted the evocation of character and place – fiction chronicles a sort of truth. Nevertheless, Aleister Crowley MI5 is a book that grew from other books and it would be unfair not to acknowledge this.

The principal source was Jean Overton Fuller's The Magical Dilemma of Victor Neuburg (Mandrake, Oxford, 1990). Fuller's book ends with a bibliography that provides much further material on what constitutes a sub-genre. Arthur Calder Marshall's The Magic of my Youth (Hart-Davis, London,1951), with its detailed account of Neuburg and Crowley, is particularly riveting.

The story of Dylan, Crowley and the doodle can be found in Constantine Fitzgibbon's Life of Dylan Thomas (Dent, London, 1975). This, along with several other biographies, sketched a portrait of the poet, which his own work, particularly The Collected Letters (Dent, London,1985), gave colour to. The Death of the King's Canary

(Hutchinson, London, 1976), co-authored with John Davenport, offered further evidence of a link between Dylan and Crowley, in addition to the references in the letters. The book satirises the literary establishment of the Thirties. Nina Hamnett, for example, appears as "Sylvia Bacon". The sinister marijuana smoking mage, "Great Raven", can only be Crowley.

Portraits of other characters were enriched by Micheal Holroyd's Augustus John (Chatto and Windus, London, 1996); Jeffrey Meyer's treatment of Wyndham Lewis, The Enemy (Routledge, London, 1980), and Francis Wheen's Tom Driberg: His Life and Indiscretions (Chatto and Windus, London, 1990). Driberg's own autobiography Ruling Passions (Quartet Books, London, 1978) proved helpful as did Augustus John's Chiaroscuro (Jonathan Cape, London. 1952), Nina Hamnett's Laughing Torso (Constable, London, 1931), and Betty May's Tiger Woman (Duckworth, London, 1929).

Several books supplied location and period detail, in particular Micheal Luke's David Tennant and the Gargoyle Years (Weidenfield, London, 1991), and Robert Graves' The Long Weekend (Abacus, London, 1995).

Another book by Constantine Fitzgibbon, Secret Intelligence in the 20th Century (Hart-Davis MacGibbon, London, 1976) furnished clues as to Crowley's role in MI5. Additional information was found in Richard Deacon's A History of the Secret Service (Muller, London, 1969); various books by Nigel West, principally MI5: British Security Service Operations (Bodley Head, London, 1981), and Antony Masters' life of Maxwell Knight, The Man Who Was M (Basil Blackwell, Oxford, 1984).

Dion Fortune's The Mystical Qabalah (Williams and Norgate, 1941), Stephen Skinner and Francis King's Techniques of Ritual Magic

(C. W. Daniel, London, 1976) helped with the magic. Israel Regardie's The Golden Dawn (Llewelyn, Saint Paul, 1984) as well as Gems from the Equinox (Falcon, Phoenix Arizona, 1984), both of which he edited, were illuminating. Regardie's biography of Crowley, Eye of the Triangle (Falcon, Phoenix Arizona, 1984), was also useful, as were various editions of John Symond's work, most notably The Magic of Aleister Crowley (Muller, London, 1958), and Martin Booth's A Magick Life (Hodder and Stoughton, London, 2000).

Of Crowley's own work, the most consulted were Magick in Theory and Practice (Routledge and Kegan Paul, London, 1973), Liber 777 (Weiser, York Beach, 1986), Magick without Tears (Falcon, Phoenix Arizona, 1982), The Confessions: an Autohagiography (Routledge, London, 1979). Correspondence with Tom Driberg alluding to mysterious liaisons and contacts was among the surprises sprung by the Gerald Yorke Collection of Crowley's writings in the Warburg Institute, London.

London, 2004

Interested in occult fiction and non fiction?
Check our website www.mandrake.uk.net

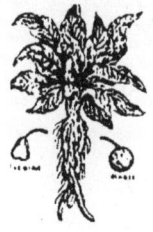

www.ingramcontent.com/pod-product-compliance
Ingram Content Group UK Ltd.
Pitfield, Milton Keynes, MK11 3LW, UK
UKHW041608060326
468719UK00004B/176